THE LAIR OF

THE DEVIL

By

Emile C. Vos

Cover Illustration by Joan Zivic

This is a work of fiction. All the characters and events portrayed In this novel are either fictitious or are used fictitiously.

THE LAIR OF THE DEVIL

First Edition

Copyright © 2000 by Emile C. Vos

Library of Congress Card Catalogue Number
00-190784

All rights reserved, including the right to reproduce this book, or portions thereof, in any form.

Published by Emile C. Vos
P.O. Box 31785
Aurora, CO 80012

www.emilecvos.com

ISBN 0-9700594-0-X

Printed in the United States of America

To Charla, for her help and advice.
To Diane, for encouraging me when I was ready to give up.
To my loving wife, for believing in me.

Thank you for helping make this possible.

THE LAIR OF THE

DEVIL

Prologue - Escape

Days had passed since it last tried to pry open the bars of the cage that held it prisoner, days of torment and hunger. Days spent in agony waiting for the effects of the hated holy water to slowly wear off, now that its caretaker was finally gone and could no longer administer the daily doses. It spent the time resting as much as possible, knowing that it was questionable whether sufficient strength and stamina would still be present after such a long period without sustenance.

It sensed the workmen in the house above, cleaning out the refuse accumulated from decades of neglect. Sensed the fresh blood that was so close, but unattainable because of the holy water. The holy water that kept the evil under control, and prevented the demon strength from shattering the prison that held it captive.

It bided its time, patiently at first, while the transformation slowly began to take place. Smooth skin, pale from lack of sunshine and outside air, turned leathery. Coarse fur, which began as small patches, grew more thickly. A feral light, barely flickering at first, radiated from the bloodshot eyes, brightening into an evil glow that filled the little cell. Ever so slowly, corded muscles formed under the fur, muscles that would allow it to tear the walls of the prison to shambles, if only they would form in time. Would starvation be the victor instead?

Then fear set in. Fear led to panic and it threw itself against the iron bars again and again, cries of bestial rage reverberating off the stone walls of the cell. The workmen above, hearing strange noises emanating from deep inside the old house paused for a moment, then hastily went back to work, convinced the old stories of the place being haunted were obviously true.

Finally, torn and bleeding, it collapsed. It lay exhausted, its dripping blood being absorbed by the dust which covered the oversized rough cut stones that made up the floor. Slowly, reason began to reassert itself. Determined not to lose control again, it crawled over to one of the walls, and painfully propped itself into a sitting position. In a barely audible whisper, it began to recite satanic prayers, focusing its mind on the repetition of the harsh guttural sounds.

Its mind numbed from the repetition, it fell asleep. Images of its past life formed in its head. Images that began with the face of a loving baby, holding its tiny arms out. Images of joy, of playing hide-and-go-seek-with a little child. Then it thrashed about as these images were splashed in blood. Another voice began to form in its mind, reminding it of the joy of killing, of the promise of power and eternal life. Abruptly it woke up. It knew that it was now or never.

Gingerly, it raised itself and walked to the iron bars, the sharp claws on its feet scraping the stones. It gripped the bars firmly. Taking a deep breath of the air reeking with the stench of refuse, it began to exert its power. The muscles on the arms and shoulders tightened under the skin, bulging from the effort.

It struggled in silence. The large blood vessels in its neck stood out as the struggle continued. Several of the smaller veins in its forehead popped, and blood mixing with sweat, ran down its face in small rivulets. It took in a sharp breath as the stinging fluid poured into its eyes.

Imperceptibly at first, the iron bars began to part. Encouraged, it increased its efforts, and the bars creaked as they slowly bent out of shape. In spite of its best efforts at self-control, a groan of agony escaped the bestial snout that made up its face. A groan that contained a human element of anguish as the pain began to build in the mighty muscles. With one last heave, the bars were torn apart. Screaming in triumph, it stepped through them. It ripped the locked wooden door to the hallway from its hinges, and made its way through the secret passageways into the house itself.

The house was shadowy with only the faint gleam of moonlight filtering in through the windows to prevent the darkness from being complete. It went to one of the basement windows, broke out the glass, and crawled out into the crisp night air. It drank in the air of freedom, exultation flowing through it like strong liquor.

Desperate for food and fresh blood, it fled across the grounds and into the woods. First it needed to gain its strength back, then if its reckoning of the passing years was correct, there would be time to deal with the boy.

PART ONE – RACHEL

Chapter One - Airborne

Randy sat poised on his bike, getting up the courage to make his attempt. Jumping over the mounds of dirt left by the construction crew on the school field had become one of his favorite activities this summer. There was a long line of mounds where a trough was dug for a new water line, which stretched from the street to the main school building. He began with the smaller mounds, only a couple of feet high, in order to get used to the sensation of being airborne with his bicycle, and to develop his balance on landing. His first few tries were less than successful, resulting in some nasty spills and a particularly ugly scrape on his right elbow that was still bandaged. The latter elicited a promise from him to his parents that he would cease doing what he continued to do ever since. It's not that Randy was disobedient by nature, on the contrary, he enjoyed a very close relationship with his parents. But like so many other twelve-year-olds, he came to the conclusion that his parents were obviously from another age. They couldn't possibly understand his need for excitement, and the thrill resulting from the possibility of crashing and the risk of serious injury. Not that Randy believed *he* could be seriously injured. Things like that happened to *other* kids who were not as lucky.

The mound he concentrated his stare on was almost eight feet tall, more than twice the height of anything he had ever attempted. He had trouble getting started. His hands clenched the handlebars as he hunched down. He tried to push off, but his feet wouldn't leave the ground. The thoughts of what the consequences could be if he did crash and his parents found out, were almost more anxiety than he could handle.

"Aw come on, Randy. Are you going to wait forever? Just do it! The worst you could do is crash, break a few bones, get in trouble with your folks, and be grounded for life." Brad was sitting impatiently on his bike, his back hunched over, with his elbows resting on the handlebars.

"Shut up, will ya. I'll do it when I'm ready. This requires concentration, something you haven't figured out yet." Randy knew he would have to make his attempt soon. The late afternoon sun was setting over the nearby mountain, and the shadow which had already engulfed the old red brick schoolhouse, rapidly approached him. The large trees overhanging the schoolyard were rustling softly in the warm afternoon breeze.

With an extreme effort, he pushed all the doubts out of his mind and began his approach. He peddled furiously. Concentrating on keeping his body low on the bike, he relaxed in order to keep his balance and improve his ability to adjust to any changes in the bike's attitude. As he neared the mound he tightened his grip on the handlebars, kept his body centered over the pedals, and tried to keep his heart from rising to his mouth. In an instant, he was propelled up over the mound and into the air. He felt he was miles above the field and would be in the air forever. The wind fanned his red hair out behind him. He exulted in the sense of freedom from being released temporarily from gravity's constraints.

He landed perfectly, his rear wheel touching ground first. The jar of being earthbound nearly threw him from the bike, but he hung on, and brought the bike to a stop. His eyes glowed with excitement and a smile stretched across his face. He let out a loud cry of victory. At that moment, he felt nothing was unattainable; everything was possible, he only had to try.

Brad rode up to him, his freckled face in awe. "I didn't think you'd make it. This must be your lucky day."

"What do you mean luck? It was pure skill. Now it's your turn."

"Hey I would, but it's getting close to dinner time, and I don't want to be home late."

Randy peddled off. "Chicken," he yelled over his shoulder. Smiling and whistling, still gripping the bars hard to stop his hands from shaking, he rode off across the schoolyard to the street. He swerved sharply when he heard Brad yell, "watch out," from behind. A passing motorist, who barely missed him, scowled sharply, her forehead furrowed in irritation. Greatly sobered, Randy cautiously began peddling home. Brad soon caught up with him, and they rode together in silence. They only lived a few blocks from the school. They rode past the older well-kept homes lining the street and began to meander back and forth down the street, the near miss with the motorist already forgotten. The huge mature trees towered over them, providing them with shade from the setting sun.

Shady Valley was not a large community. It was a small mountain town with approximately 5,000 inhabitants. There had not been a great deal of new construction within the last several years, so the town had a quaint, older appearance to it. It had first been settled in the late 1800's when it had started out as a mining community.

Randy turned into the driveway of the old Humphries' mansion.

"Hey," yelled Brad bringing his bike to a screeching stop. "Are you crazy? We can't go that way."

"Why not? Old man Humphries is gone and there's no one living here now. Besides, if you'll look at the real estate sign by the road, you'll see my parents' name on it. They have the listing on the place." Randy put his head back slightly, "so I have every right to come this way."

"I don't know, the place gives me the creeps."

"Aw come on, Brad. I don't want to ride all the way around. I'm hungry. And remember, I saw them take the old man out with my own eyes. They hauled him out tied to a stretcher. He was squirming around like some nut, yelling that his job wasn't done yet, that it was still alive."

"I wonder what he meant by that?"

"Oh who knows. The man was crazy. The only time we ever saw him, was every Sunday when he went to church over there." Randy nodded to the Roman Catholic church across the street that his family attended. "They ended up locking him away in some nursing home."

Leading the way, Randy rode up the driveway towards the house. The multiple acre estate was located on the edge of the small mountain community, and butted up against the woods surrounding the town. Resembling an old gothic castle, the three-story structure with its square corner turrets seemed completely out of place with the community that sprang up around it. The large oversized gray stones gave it a somber, macabre appearance. The six foot tall windows, many of which were arched, seemed to regard visitors with an air of disdain, giving people the impression of having wandered into a different time that had passed by long ago. Old, gnarled trees surrounded the house on all sides, and lined the long, 200 yard driveway that led up to the house. The driveway split off in two directions. One branch went past the side of the mansion to the carriage house, and the other curved around to the entry-way that jutted out from the porch which extended across the front of the building. Life-sized stone lions guarded the broad, massive stone steps that led up to the ten-foot tall double doors. Large arched windows directly above provided an almost cathedral-like appearance.

"The place sure looks cleaned up," Brad remarked as he looked side to side. "All the weeds are gone."

"Yeah, my folks hired a bunch of people to knock it into shape. I gather the inside was filled with cockroaches and rats. It took them two weeks just to haul all the trash away."

As they were riding on the driveway past the side of the house, Randy noticed that one of the basement windows was broken. Stopping, he got off his bike and took a closer look. "Hey Brad, take a look at this."

Brad had continued onward, but came back around. "Yeah, it's only a broken window."

With a sweep of his arm, Randy put on his Sherlock Holmes imitation. "On the contrary, my dear Watson, you will note that the glass is broken out from the inside. That alone should give one pause for thought. What force could possibly accomplish such an act? After all, if you will recall, the house is presumed to be vacant. And if you would be so kind as to take a closer look at these tracks, you will note that they are extremely unusual. I must confess, I myself have never seen anything like them." Randy was very well read, and possessed vocabulary and speech patterns that even surpassed most of the adults he came in contact with.

"Aw, cut it out Randy, quit showing off. Act normal, will ya? Okay, so the tracks are a little bigger than I've ever seen. Maybe they were made by a bear or something. Can we please go? I need to get home. I still gotta pack after dinner. Remember, I'm leaving with my folks for vacation tomorrow."

Randy moved the pieces of broken glass around with his foot. "I suppose I'll have to tell my folks about this, so they can get it fixed." He fell silent for a moment, staring at the ground. "You know, I'm gonna miss you."

"I'm only gonna be gone for a couple of weeks. Don't tell me you're gonna get all mushy on me. You want a goodbye hug to keep you goin' until I get back?"

"Oh shut up and let's go!" Randy rode off quickly, not looking back to see if Brad was following. He raced past the old carriage house, and sped across the grounds to the back gate. He was about to go through it when he heard Brad come puffing up behind him.

"Hey, hold up." Brad pulled up next to him. "You know? I'll miss you too." With that, Brad turned his bike and continued along the fence to his own home.

Randy smiled as he went through the gate into his backyard. He looked up at his house as he got off his bike. At one time, the house had actually been the guesthouse of the Humphries' estate. His parents purchased the property from old man Humphries when they first got married. The old man had made it clear that he had no wish to sell the house, but that his financial situation at the time forced the issue. The guesthouse was a total contrast to the main building. Whereas the main building seemed haughty and intimidating, the smaller guesthouse was quaint and cheerful. The single story house was constructed of much smaller, lighter-colored stones, which combined with the wooden shingle roof, gave the property a friendly welcoming look. Other than the screened in back porch, not much of the guesthouse could be seen from the back yard. The house had considerable depth, with most of the rooms opening off the main hallway that ran down the middle of the interior to the kitchen.

Randy parked his bike by the back door to the garage that had been added to the side of the house, adjacent to the back porch. He turned to pet his dog Thunder, who had gotten up from the shade under the tree and lumbered over to greet his friend. Even for a Saint Bernard, Thunder was unusually large, weighing in at close to 240 pounds. His enormous square head mounted on broad shoulders gave the animal a majestic appearance that was further enhanced by the full, black mask that surrounded his eyes. Randy scratched Thunder behind one of his ears, and the large animal responded by stretching out his legs and giving a little growl of pleasure. The dog leaned into Randy, hoping that the attention he was getting would last for awhile. Randy was hungry, however, and anxious to find out what was for dinner. He gave Thunder a big hug, and ran in the back door into the kitchen.

"Randy, you certainly look excited. What did you do this afternoon?" Wearing a red and white plaid cotton apron, his mother was standing by the large gas stove stirring a pan of gravy.

The kitchen was one of the few rooms in the house that had been significantly modernized. Even though Randy's parents enjoyed the rustic atmosphere the old guesthouse provided, they felt that when it came to the kitchen, functionality had to be the number one priority. The kitchen was quite large, measuring in at twelve by twenty feet. Stainless steel commercial grade units had replaced all the outdated appliances. Both of Randy's parents liked to cook and entertain, and enjoyed being able to prepare gourmet meals. All the cabinets were custom-made from dark cherry wood, and combined with the light blue flowered wallpaper and cream colored ceramic tiled floor, provided a pleasing color contrast. The kitchen was also the only room in the house where the ceiling had been lowered from ten feet to eight feet. This allowed the contractor to install the additional lighting and ductwork necessary to satisfy modern standards. Randy sat down at the cherry dinette set that was placed at one end of the kitchen.

"Oh, just rode around the neighborhood, nothing special." Randy was irritated that his mother always seemed to sense whenever something different was afoot. "Oh, pot-roast, one of my favorites. You sure are a great cook, Mom." He hoped to change the subject away from the day's activities, and figured a little compliment might help to do so.

"Everything is your favorite, as long as it's food. Now hurry and get washed up. Your father will be home soon, and you still need to get the table set for dinner."

His mother wasn't fooled the slightest bit, but felt the issue wasn't worth pursuing. Randy was basically a good son in her opinion, and she realized that as a twelve-year-old, he would want to feel a little in control of his life from time to time. Ellen, Randy's mother, had the benefit of a little more maturity to help her raise Randy. She and Jake, Randy's father, had married in their late twenties. Even though they had both desired to have children, nothing happened for several years. Randy had not arrived until Ellen was well into her thirties. The pregnancy and childbirth had been rough on her. Being slight of build, and barely reaching five feet, four inches, in heels, she certainly did not give the appearance of being able to give birth to a nine-pound baby boy. Having inherited his father's stature, Randy was already his mother's size, and enjoyed teasing her about it. Randy definitely had his mother's red hair, but looked like his father in almost every other way. He was both very tall and broad, and gave the impression of being much older than he was.

"Randy," Ellen said as Randy returned to set the table, "your father and I have to present an offer to the Claytons on their house tonight, and we're not sure when we'll get back. Will you be okay by yourself tonight?"

"Sure, Mom," Randy was relieved that he had managed to re-focus her attention. "But they're showing *Star Wars* on TV tonight, and I was looking forward to watching it."

"Dad!" he exclaimed as his father walked into the kitchen. "It's too bad we won't be able to watch *Star Wars* together."

Jake sat down wearily at the kitchen table. Being a big man, over six feet in height, and 260 pounds in weight, he detested the restricted feel of a business suit, and had already taken his coat and tie off. Small beads of sweat had formed on his partially bald head, and his blue eyes looked tired. It was hard to tell what his original hair color had been, since the remaining hair on his head, along with his beard and mustache, had turned prematurely gray some years ago.

"I take it your mother gave you the bad news. Sorry, son, I was looking forward to it as much as you were. Unfortunately, we wrote an offer on the Clayton property this afternoon, and it has to be presented this evening. As much trouble as we've been having selling their house, I don't want to lose any opportunities. If we get it sold, then after closing we'll rent the entire trilogy, and I'll take a day off just so that we can watch it together." Jake reached over and roughed up Randy's hair.

"So be prepared Luke Skywalker, Darth Vader will defeat you yet," warned Jake as he and Randy began a mock light-saber fight. Randy and his father had a very special relationship. From the time of Randy's birth, his father had taken as much time as possible to be a major player in Randy's upbringing, oftentimes at the expense of career and business. He didn't mind the sacrifices one bit, however. He thoroughly enjoyed being with his son, and hoped the closeness would continue on into the dreaded teen years.

Ellen walked up carrying a hot pan with potholders. "I hate to break up your life and death battle, but unless you warriors are intent on skipping dinner, I suggest you finish setting the table."

Randy hurriedly finished setting the table. His mother put the food on the table, and they all sat down to dinner. Randy dug in voraciously, the aroma of the pot roast wetting his appetite. He always demonstrated an ability to pack away enormous quantities of food for someone as slender as he was. His father, however, being heavy in spite of watching his diet, was envious.

"Randy," his father admonished, "if you keep eating like that you're going to get as big as me. And believe me, you don't want to do that. Not only does the extra weight slow you down, but clothes are outrageously expensive when you have to get the extra-big sizes."

"Randy," said his mother softly. "I was trying to clean up the study today, when I noticed that the desk was a complete mess. All the family correspondence and letters looked like someone had gone through them and then just stuffed them back into the drawers. Do you know anything about that?"

"No, Mom, I don't. I haven't been in the study in days. There's usually no reason for me to go in there."

"Well, from now on, I don't want to see you in the study at all. You know that if there's something you need, all you have to do is ask."

"Oh, I almost forgot," said Randy, wanting to change the subject, "I was cutting through the Humphries' property on the way home, and *please,* I know I'm not supposed to, and I'm sorry," Randy quickly interjected when he saw his parents' faces get very stern, "but I figured you would probably want to know that I found a broken basement window by the driveway. Strange thing was that it looked like something had broken out rather than in. The glass was scattered outward, and there were animal tracks leading away from the window."

"I think we're going to regret ever having taken that listing," sighed Randy's father wearily. "Not only is the place going to be a pain to sell, I suspect it's going to be a constant headache with incidents like this. I'll bet that when the work crew was in there last week they probably had the doors open while they were busy hauling out the garbage and some animal slipped in and got trapped inside. One of us will have to check it out tomorrow. Hon, what's your schedule look like?"

"I can't, my day is completely booked with appointments, sorry."

"Well, I guess I'll have to try to take a look at it sometime in the afternoon," Randy's father said with a resigned sigh.

Randy looked up from his plate. "Dad, why is the place going to be so hard to sell? It's kind of a neat old house, even if it does look a little spooky."

"Everyone in town is convinced it's haunted. They all figure that the ghost of the servant that was murdered there over fifty years ago roams the property. And it certainly didn't help when those relatives of Humphries tried to move in and only stayed one night. Unless we find some out-of-town buyers that aren't so ridiculously superstitious, it'll never sell."

"But wasn't the murder supposed to be some kind of satanic ritual performed by Humphries' mother?"

"Randy, no one knows what happened for sure, and after fifty years, everyone's imaginations have blown the entire affair way out of proportion. Now will you please drop it? The last thing we need now, is for you to start spreading fresh rumors around with all your buddies."

After dinner, Randy went into the family room and turned on the home theater system to watch *Star Wars* while his parents cleaned up and got ready to leave. The theater system was a source of pride and joy for both Randy and his father. They had gutted the entire room, and totally remodeled it to accommodate the various gargantuan speaker systems that filled the room. At first, Ellen complained whenever the system was turned up too loud, but she soon resigned herself to the fact that from time to time the house would rock from the sounds of passing dinosaurs, or jet fighter planes roaring through.

As soon as Thunder was through with his dinner, he came over and lay down next to Randy who had sat on the floor with his back to the couch. Thunder gently lay his head in Randy's lap, and snored contentedly as Randy scratched behind his ear. Even though Randy had seen *Star Wars* numerous times, he never tired of it. He watched the entire movie while constantly making editorial comments to Thunder. Randy also told Thunder all about the day's events, and the big dog fulfilled his part of the ritual by knowing precisely when to voice a soft growl of approval, or look up at Randy with an understanding look in his dark brown eyes.

After the movie, Randy realized he was more tired than he thought, and got ready to go to bed. With the sound of a light rain coming in through the window, he fell asleep shortly after lying down. Thunder stretched out at the foot of the bed in his usual spot.

In the middle of the night Randy woke up, feeling chilled. Acting on a sudden premonition, he turned quickly, and saw a shadow at the window. Darker than the night sky surrounding it, the shadow seemed to hover at the window. Randy was about to let out a yell, when Thunder raised his head and let out a low growl. Instantly, the shadow disappeared. Still shaking, and with Thunder at his side, he cautiously approached the window and looked out. Stare as he might, he could find nothing out of the ordinary. He tried to convince himself that it had only been his imagination, but nevertheless, it took some time before he was able to get back to sleep.

Chapter Two - Rachel

The sun was already shining brightly into the room when Randy woke up. The smell of the early morning air filled the room. He had not slept well the remainder of the night, having experienced nightmares of demonic images chasing him down twisted hallways and corridors. The dreams were all but forgotten in the morning light, but left him with an uneasy feeling he could not shake.

Randy had always been very sensitive from early childhood on. He was very adept at tuning into other people's emotions and possessed an uncanny ability to instinctively discern other people's thoughts, when he made the effort. Although not clairvoyant, his parents learned to pay attention to his feelings about the future. Randy was not able to predict the future as such, but seemed to have a sense of general direction, be it good or ill. He was not aware of being different from others. He just naturally assumed everyone was like himself. His parents never made the issue a topic of discussion, as they did not wish to encourage any egotistical feelings on Randy's part.

Randy rolled out of bed and made his way down to the bathroom for a quick shower. Since he was not by nature a morning person, he always found a hot shower the best way to wake up in the morning. After returning to his room refreshed, he dressed, and headed to the kitchen for breakfast. Since it was already mid-morning, he was surprised to find his mother still at home.

"Good morning, Randy," his mother said as he walked into the kitchen. "Look who's here, your cousin Rachel. She'll be staying with us for a few days."

Rachel was the daughter of Jake's brother. Since Jake was not very close to his brother, they never saw a great deal of Rachel. Indeed, it had been a good six months since the blond-haired, petite six-year-old last visited them. Rachel was always very quiet and difficult to talk to. She would politely respond to any questions put to her, but would do so in a very brief manner that made further discussion difficult.

Randy turned to the table to say hello just as Rachel looked up at him. As their eyes met, Randy felt a shiver go down his spine. Rachel's blue eyes did not look any different than usual, but seemed colder. The sense of foreboding that Randy had felt when he got up suddenly intensified beyond anything he had ever experienced. He managed a shaky "Hi," and sat down at the table.

"Are you all right this morning?" asked his mother. "You look a little pale."

"Yeah, I'm okay, just a little tired." Randy answered almost absent-mindedly as he turned to look at Rachel a little more closely. The little girl was quietly eating her scrambled eggs and certainly did not appear unusual in any way. And yet, Randy felt uneasy. He sensed something was wrong about her although he couldn't explain why.

"Where are Uncle Bill and Aunt Becky?" Randy asked curiously.

"They're not here," his mother responded while wiping the counter. "When we got up this morning we found Rachel sitting on the front porch waiting for us. She had a note with her from Uncle Bill asking us if we could take care of her for a few days. It appears that Aunt Becky had a family emergency that forced them to take off immediately. Since they didn't want to wake us up super early in the morning, they figured it would be okay to drop Rachel off here on their way out of town."

"That must be some emergency," Randy said in-between bites. "Did the note say what it was?"

"No it didn't. Aunt Becky's always been somewhat quiet about her family. Who knows why."

"Even so, just dropping Rachel off here by herself seems a little strange, don't you think?" Randy guzzled down half of his orange juice.

"Well I suppose it does." She paused as if in thought, then added, "I'm sure everything's all right."

Randy couldn't help but notice that during his mother's pause, Rachel looked up and seemed to be staring quite intently at his mother. It wasn't until his mother stated that everything was all right that Rachel turned her attention back to her breakfast. Randy couldn't shake the feeling that something was wrong, but he sensed that his mother was not going to be the key to solving this mystery. She seemed too distant this morning.

"Rachel, did your mom say what was wrong?" Randy whispered quietly.

Suddenly, Randy's glass of orange juice fell over and spilled over the table into his lap. Rachel burst into tears. Randy's mother, seeing what had happened, grabbed some paper towels, and rushed over to the table to clean up the mess and console Rachel.

"For heaven's sake Randy, let it drop," his mother hissed. "Can't you see that Rachel is upset? I had to rearrange my entire day, move all my appointments around, just so I could be here today. I don't need you to make matters worse. Go back to your room and put on some dry clothes. And please, leave Rachel alone, and keep Thunder outside! Remember, Rachel doesn't like dogs." She then turned her attention to the little girl crying behind a plate of scrambled eggs swimming in orange juice.

Bewildered, Randy headed back to his room to put on some dry clothes. The whole affair just didn't make sense. No matter how strange Uncle Bill and Aunt Becky were, it was odd for anyone to leave a six-year-old on someone's doorstep; even for them. He thought he might tackle his dad later in the afternoon when he got home. In the meantime, he wondered where this "note" was and what it looked like.

Randy found some clean clothes in his room, despite his room looking like the aftermath of a tornado passing through. Even though the room had plenty of closet and drawer space, Randy was not the world's tidiest individual. His parents had done their best to encourage his taking "ownership" of his bedroom by allowing him to pick his own furnishings, but all to no avail. It's not that he was unhappy with the room; on the contrary, he very much enjoyed his domain. The large king-size waterbed tended to dominate the medium-sized room, but the oak furniture gave it a rustic look that Randy felt belonged in the house.

Randy poked his head out of the window into the backyard to see how Thunder was doing. He hated to see Thunder stuck outside for the duration of Rachel's visit, but realized there was no choice. Rachel's parents were themselves unused to dogs, and like so many other people, learned to fear them out of ignorance. Unfortunately, they did an excellent job of communicating this fear to their daughter, teaching her that all dogs were bad and to be distrusted. Rachel always screamed out whenever Thunder got anywhere close to her. Thunder, in turn, would react curiously to the screaming, wanting to sniff Rachel to check out what was wrong. Unless Rachel had an opportunity to "un-learn" her fear of dogs, the two would never get along.

As Randy put his head out of the window, he noticed strange animal tracks in the wet dirt below. They reminded him of the tracks he had seen outside the broken window at the Humphries' mansion.

He looked up to see Thunder asleep under the large elm tree in the back yard. Randy decided he should console his friend and at the same time check out the strange tracks. He pulled his head back into his room and headed for the back door.

As he walked down the hall, he went by the guestroom and saw his mother helping Rachel into bed, letting the little girl get some rest after her early morning.

"Mom, I'm sorry about the mess I made. If it's okay, I'd like to go out bike riding."

His mother tucked Rachel into bed, and came to the door. "Just be careful, and don't go too far," she said softly.

Thunder lazily raised his head and wagged his tail as Randy came over to sit down next to him. Randy leaned over to give Thunder a big hug, then leaned with his back against the tree while scratching Thunder on top of his head. He looked up into the tree and saw the tree house that he and his father built together some years ago. He enjoyed the memories of helping his father build it. His father never did anything half way. The rope ladder coming out of the bottom led up into the main room, with a second room on the other side of the tree trunk. There was a ladder attached to the trunk which led upward to the observation deck. From up there you could see most of the neighborhood spread out below. The entire structure was solidly built, with opening glass windows, and was even insulated. He and his father spent many nights up there together.

Randy gave Thunder a final pat on the head, left the dog napping in the shade, and got up to check out the animal tracks by his window. They were deep with sharply defined claw marks on them. They were like nothing Randy had ever seen. Living on the outskirts of a mountain community, he was used to seeing wild animal tracks, but not usually in the town itself, and nothing like these. He followed the tracks to the front porch of the house, but could not find where they led from there. He supposed the animal could have left by the sidewalk. He decided to backtrack. He followed them out through the back gate of the yard, onto the Humphries' property, and across the large estate into the woods beyond. He soon lost track of the prints in the undergrowth, but decided to follow the general direction for a while for lack of anything better to do.

It was a warm day, but not so hot as to be uncomfortable. The sky was the deep blue that can only be seen in the mountains. A gentle breeze carried the sounds of the birds softly chirping. The trees formed a nice canopy overhead, providing a pleasantly shaded environment underneath. He took a deep breath of the pine scented air, and was enjoying the peace and quiet of the surroundings, when he stepped into a clearing and froze at the sight of the scene ahead of him.

The remains of a fairly good-sized deer that been attacked and killed by a predator, lay before him. The unfortunate deer was torn limb from limb. There were various portions of the body spread about the small clearing, all shredded to ribbons. Randy glanced down at his feet and saw the deer's head lying on the ground. It was torn from the rest of the body. He couldn't help but notice the eyes, still filled with a mixture of surprise and terror. He turned aside and became suddenly ill from the sight and smell of fresh blood. He retched several times before he regained control of himself. He ran back towards home, crying as he went, unable to get the sight of the deer's eyes out of his mind.

    Exhaustion finally forced him to slow down. He started to think about what he should do. If something dangerous was on the loose this close to town, people had to be warned. He decided to go talk to Fred, the town sheriff. He and Fred were good friends. Fred and his father had been close since before Randy was born. Fred was familiar with the wildlife of the area, and would have a much better idea of what had caused the horrible scene.

Chapter Three - The Map

Fred was sitting at his desk doing the one thing he disliked the most: paperwork. Unfortunately, it seemed his job was turning more and more into paper shuffling. As the years went by, the list of reports required by the various government agencies just kept growing. Fred had been sheriff of Shady Valley for ten years. The part of the job he liked most was being in touch with the people. Fred loved being part of the entire community. Since he was divorced several years ago, and never had any children, he considered the townspeople his extended family. He enjoyed being able to help take care of them. Since Shady Valley was an extremely quiet town, Fred's job was generally laid back.

In an effort to make paperwork as pleasant as possible, Fred took great pains to make his office an enjoyable place to be. The large desk dominated the office, but was turned so his back was against the wall and he could see out the window. The office was on the main street of the town, with the town's only park just across the street. A small stream ran through the park with large trees on the banks. Fred enjoyed being able to glance at it from time to time in order to relax.

The desk, gun cabinet, and file cabinets were all antique in appearance. Ornate carvings and moldings graced the dark stained oak. Since the wooden doors, door posts, and crown molding were painted when Fred took possession of the office, he had spent untold hours stripping away the paint, restoring the natural wood finish.

Fred was startled as the door flew open and Randy exploded into the office. Fred always kept a special place in his heart for Randy. Fred and Jake had been close friends since the time they met in college. Fred settled in Shady Valley soon after graduation, and convinced Jake and Ellen to move there a few years later. When Randy was born, Fred treated him as his own son, but without the barriers that a parental relationship can sometimes create. The result was that Randy oftentimes confided things to him that he wouldn't dream of telling his own parents.

Sweat poured from Randy's head and arms, and his eyes appeared red and swollen from crying. Gasping for breath, his face was pale and withdrawn.

Fred looked him over. "What happened to you? You look like you've just been chased by a grizzly bear."

Randy didn't respond right away, but sat down on the chair by Fred's desk, trying to compose himself. He grabbed the glass of water on the desk and took several large gulps.

"Help yourself. I always leave a glass of water there in case you come running in." After studying Randy more closely, Fred started to become concerned. "Hey, it's okay. Settle down." He sensed that Randy was genuinely terrified. "What happened?"

"I was following some animal tracks I found by the side of our house," Randy spoke slowly, still gasping for breath. "I followed them into the woods, and lost track of them when I found a deer that had been killed. Fred, it was awful. Whatever did it just tore that deer to pieces. You've got to go see."

"Why don't you show me on the map where it happened."

Fred had a large topographical map of the area on one of the walls of his office. Still shaking, Randy got to his feet and went over to it with Fred behind, ready to steady him. Randy studied the map for a while and pointed to where he thought the clearing was, just to the north of town. Fred looked at the spot. He saw there was a four-wheel drive trail that passed very close to the area Randy pointed to.

"Come on, Randy, let's go for a ride." Fred led Randy out the door to the Jeep that was parked out front. Even though he doubted that the situation was as serious as Randy seemed to think, he appreciated the excuse to get out of the office for awhile. Fred loved the outdoors and enjoyed any reason for taking the Jeep onto the trails that wandered into the mountains surrounding the town. Since the weather was usually cooperative, he almost always had the top of the Jeep down so he could enjoy the mountain air.

Fred was tall; almost six foot, four inches, and relatively slim, which irritated his friends. He had an enormous appetite, and never seemed to gain the weight one would expect for the amounts he consumed. He kept his dark hair short and neat, contributing to a youthful, athletic appearance.

He quickly sped down the few roads that led to the trail, then was forced to stop in order to put the Jeep in low range. The trail was much worse than Fred remembered. Large rocks had rolled into the pathway, and deep holes had formed in several places.

As he began to ease the vehicle across the rough terrain, he was surprised at Randy's silence. Randy was usually a non-stop talker, and found keeping quiet to be difficult under any circumstance. Whatever spooked him did an exceptional job.

The trail was narrow, and it took all of Fred's concentration to keep from hitting the trees that were on both sides of the trail. Even so, the clearing Randy pointed out was not far from the town, and it didn't take very long to get there.

Fred stepped out of the Jeep. "All right, if I read the map right, your clearing should be just through those trees on the right."

Fred led the way. It was difficult going through the tangled underbrush, and although Fred was in fairly good shape, he found himself working up a sweat. They went perhaps a hundred yards, when they stepped into the clearing.

Even Fred, who spent a great deal of time outdoors, was surprised by what he saw. Not only was the carcass shredded far beyond what was necessary to make the kill, there were even bloody bits of fur hanging from the branches above the clearing. The clearing was only about twenty feet across, with the main portion of the carcass off to one side. He knelt down to take a closer look. He spread apart the slashes and found they were about two inches deep, with clean-cut edges.

"Whatever did this sure has some long sharp claws. Randy, come over and take a look at these tracks by the body. They don't look familiar to me at all."

Randy stepped hesitantly over to Fred and took a look at the tracks. He shivered despite the warm sun. The tracks were almost five inches across, and extra deep, as though made by an unusually heavy animal. The claw indentations were sharp and well defined, leaving deep impressions in the ground. The pad portion of the prints were longer than usual, however, making the symmetry appear somewhat unusual for an animal.

"They're identical to the ones I found outside my bedroom window."

Fred turned the body over and found the entire underside ripped open. He carefully opened the giant gash and shuddered at what he found. In total contrast to the carnage that was wrecked on the rest of the body, he found that the animal's heart had been removed with almost surgical precision. Whatever killed with such frightful frenzy was also capable of cool and precise actions. Fred followed the tracks leading from the clearing, but soon lost them when they led onto rocky ground.

"I have to admit, I've never seen tracks like these. I haven't the slightest idea what made them. I'm concerned that they're the same as the ones you found by your house. Granted, you guys do live close to the edge of town, but most wild animals avoid humans as much as possible."

"And I also saw them by the Humphries house. Yesterday, on the way home, I was cutting through the estate when I noticed a broken window. There were tracks like these just outside it."

"The Humphries house," mused Fred, "now that's interesting. Just last month, I was trying to get together some of the older files, so I could archive them, and came across the file on the Humphries' murder investigation. For as much publicity as the case got, there's surprisingly little in the file. The only really interesting thing in there was an old map. Then just yesterday, I got a call from the nursing home where Humphries is being kept. It seems they want me to talk to him. They said he's genuinely afraid of something, but that he won't talk to them about it. They're hoping that maybe a visit from the sheriff will be official enough that he'll open up.

"Well, I think we've seen everything there is to see up here. We're both hot and thirsty. Why don't we go back to my place, have something cold to drink, and come up with a plan of action."

That was one of the things Randy liked about Fred. Instead of treating him like a child, Fred always kept him involved, even when things got exciting.

The whole way back, both Fred and Randy were quiet, each one busy with thoughts of the morning's events. The ride back to town was uneventful, and Fred went directly to his home only a few blocks from his office. It was a relatively small house, narrow at the front, with a second story rising up midway back. Constructed mostly out of red brick, the house had a solid look about it despite its obvious age. Fred loved the past, and enjoyed studying the history of the town and surrounding area. He sometimes wished he had lived a hundred years ago in what appeared to have been a simpler, less complex lifestyle.

After parking the Jeep in the driveway, Fred led Randy in through the side entrance and down the hallway to the back of the house where he kept his study. There was a large oak desk in the center of the room, surrounded with bookshelves on all the available walls. A fireplace off to one side gave the room a rustic appearance, with old west artifacts on the mantle above. The entire room looked like it came out of the 1800's.

Fred motioned for Randy to sit in the chair by the fireplace while he went to the kitchen for cold sodas. Randy settled in the over-stuffed chair, and wiggled a little to make himself comfortable. He glanced at the table next to him, and noticed an old map on it. It was hand written in Spanish, and was jagged on one edge, as if it had been torn out of a book. He picked it up very carefully, as it appeared stiff and brittle with age.

"What does that look like to you," asked Fred, as he walked back in with the sodas.

Randy looked at it closely, taking note of the placement of the mountains, and the stream running through the middle. "It's a map of this valley! But how old is it? There's certainly no town on it."

"That's the map I found in the Humphries' file. There was no explanation as to what it is or where it was found. I had someone from the university take a look at it. It dates back to the time of the first Spanish explorers who came through this valley. If you'll notice, there appears to be a cave mouth here on the map that would end up being somewhere in town. The map is labeled *guarida del diablo*, which was the name the Spanish had given this valley. The town folks who later settled here were uncomfortable with that, so they renamed it Shady Valley."

"What does that mean, *guarida del diablo*."

"Lair of the devil," answered Fred, lowering the tone of his voice in an attempt to sound dramatic.

Randy squirmed. The bright sunshine streaming in through the window did nothing to help lift the darkness that seemed to form inside the room.

"I wouldn't be concerned," assured Fred. "The Spanish explorers of the time were more than slightly superstitious, and tended to explain everything in terms of the supernatural."

"Fred, how did the murder take place at the Humphries house fifty years ago. I asked Dad, but he wouldn't talk about it."

"I'm not surprised. Your father's always worried about anything that might harm the town's image. Afraid it might be bad for business."

"I promise I won't tell anyone else. Can't you tell me something about it?"

Fred gave Randy a long look. "Well all right, but keep it under your hat. Even I don't know a lot. Like I said, the file has precious little information on what's probably the most notorious murder that's ever taken place in this state."

Fred took a long drink from his soda before continuing. "As you know, the murder victim was one of the Humphries' servants. It seems that Rachel Humphries, the mother of old man Humphries, was the prime suspect. A lot of witnesses said that she was deeply involved in Satanism and the occult, and killed the servant in the performance of some satanic ritual. There was never enough evidence to indict her, and she disappeared shortly after the murder. Her husband committed suicide a few years after, and their son lived in the house all alone until he was pulled out a few weeks ago."

Randy squirmed in the chair, his arms wrapped around himself. "What do we do now?"

"*We* are going to do nothing. *You* are going to go home and keep this to yourself until I find out more about what's going on. First I'll put out the word that there may be a dangerous animal prowling about in the woods, so hopefully, people will be on their guard. Then, I'm going to go back to the clearing, collect the remains of that animal along with castings of the predator's tracks, and take them into Mesa Springs to be analyzed. Since this is likely to take a few days, I expect you to stay home, out of the woods, and out of trouble. Understood?"

"Understood," replied Randy.

Outside, the sun passed behind a cloud, and Randy shivered as the room grew darker.

Chapter Four - The Cemetery

Randy headed back home as Fred had suggested. He was famished, and hoped that he would find his mom at home so she could make him something special for lunch. He was not that lucky, however. He found a note on the kitchen table from his mother saying that she and Rachel had gone shopping, and were going to have a picnic lunch in the park afterwards. The note invited Randy to join them, but he decided not to. Normally he would, but Rachel made him feel uncomfortable, and the less time he spent with her, the better he liked it.

He made himself a couple of sandwiches with some left over roast beef he found in the refrigerator, and felt much better. Since Rachel was not in the house, he let Thunder join him for company. The big dog was only too happy to come in. Randy was a soft touch, and Thunder's sad, puppy dog expression was always good for lots of table scraps.

After lunch, Randy tried to find something to do around the house, but soon found himself bored. Also, he could not get the business about the animal tracks by the Humphries' house out of his mind. Rousing Thunder, he took the dog with him to check out the tracks. Certainly Fred wouldn't mind him checking things out in the middle of the afternoon.

He walked across the estate with Thunder at his side. The dog was large enough that Randy could occasionally reach down and pet him without having to bend over. He went directly to the broken window, hoping to pick up the tracks. He found them easily enough, but they quickly led to some rocky ground where he lost them. He tried to coax Thunder into tracking by scent, but the dog had never been trained to do anything of the sort. Thunder only wagged his tail as Randy tried to demonstrate by getting on his hands and knees, and sniffing the ground.

Discouraged, Randy wandered aimlessly around the grounds. He had never been able to explore the area so thoroughly before, so he decided he might as well take advantage of the opportunity.

He was over on the far north side of the estate when he spied an area that was walled off, and went over to investigate. The wall was over ten feet tall, too tall for him to climb. Vines had so covered the wall, that it was almost impossible to see the large gray stones from which it had been constructed. There were several fragments of stones along the base of the wall that had chipped away over the years. Thick spider webs filled in many of the areas between the vines, and Randy backed away when he saw several shiny black spiders patiently waiting for their prey. He followed the wall to an iron gate that was set in the corner. He had to fumble with the rusty latch for some time before he was able to work it loose. With a loud creak, he opened it, and went in.

The area inside was fairly large, some thirty feet square. Even though remnants of rose vines clung to the walls, testimony to a past when the area must have been a beautiful garden, everything was now overrun with weeds. Rotted wooden beams that had once been a gazebo, lay twisted on the ground, infested with ants that were busy scurrying over them. A path had been made which Randy followed, Thunder at his heels. He stopped short when he came to a set of gravestones. He suddenly sobered when he realized this must have been the family cemetery. He studied the names and dates, and decided the two stones on the left:

JOSEPH RICHARD   MARTHA LOUISE
   HUMPHRIES   HUMPHRIES
   1832 - 1901   1852 - 1880

were from the grandfather and grandmother, while the single stone on the right must have been Humphries' father:

JOSEPH RICHARD
HUMPHRIES, II
1880 - 1949

    Randy stood quietly for a while, saddened that the entire area had fallen into such a state of disrepair. He hoped that who ever purchased the estate would clean up and maintain the cemetery.
    He turned to leave when his eye caught a glimpse of something shiny in the weeds. He stepped over to take a look, and found a small gold medallion on a chain that had fallen in the dirt. The chain was broken, and Randy thought it must have fallen from the owner's neck. Probably old man Humphries, he concluded.
    He looked at it closely, and found an angel engraved on one side of it, with an inscription in a different language on the

other. It seemed valuable, and he was sure Humphries would want it back, but how to get it to him? If he went to his father, he'd get in trouble for poking around on the estate. If he went to Fred, he'd get in trouble for not staying out of things until Fred got back.

He thought for a while, and decided to visit Father Brian at the church. Not only would Father be able to get it back to Humphries, he could do so without getting Randy in trouble. He might also be able to find out more about the medallion. Just holding it gave him a sense of peace that he found quite addicting.

Father Brain was busy pulling weeds. His garden was his pride and joy, and he tried to spend at least an hour a day keeping it neat and orderly. He was trying to remove the ever-intrusive weeds from the neat rows of flowers, and stopped a moment to wipe the perspiration from his brow. In his previous parish, he would never have had the opportunity to indulge himself this way. That parish had been large, too large, he reflected. There were always too many demands on too few available hours. If he wasn't being constantly called on for some emergency, he was busy trying to keep the politics of a large parish under control. He was in his late fifties now, and after dealing with all that for six years, he was happy to receive his assignment in Shady Valley. It was like being rewarded with a vacation.

His parish consisted of only fifty families, and was close knit enough to be one large family. He knew everyone in the small town, and was well liked by all, Catholics and non-Catholics alike.

He was surprised to see Randy come walking across the street towards him. He knew the family well enough, and had been invited over to their house occasionally for dinner. But try as he might, he could not get them to practice their faith more consistently. Jake and Ellen both seemed to have a deep faith in God, but just didn't see any need to celebrate that faith within the structure of the church. Father Brian got to his feet as Randy walked up to him with Thunder at his side.

"Hello Randy, what brings you my way on this beautiful afternoon?" Fr. Brian genuinely liked Randy. Randy struck him as being a real person, content to just be himself, not constantly trying to conform to his peer's expectations, as so many youths seemed to do. Randy also seemed particularly insightful in matters of faith. He didn't often ask questions of Father Brian, but when he did, Father Brian was always surprised at how Randy instinctively knew how to get to the heart of any issue that was on his mind.

"I'm sorry to bother you, Father, but I found this medallion over on the grounds of the Humphries estate. I assume it belonged to Mr. Humphries, and I was hoping you might be able to get it back to him. It looks valuable."

He handed it to Father Brian who held it up to take a good look at it. "Yes, I remember this medallion well. Mr. Humphries brought it to me a couple of years ago and asked me to bless it. He hoped it would protect him from evil. I explained to him that the only things that would protect him from evil, were his faith and prayer. If the medallion helped remind him of his faith, and helped him to focus his prayers, then yes, it would help protect him from evil. He seemed to find that reassuring, and thanked me for blessing it." He paused for a moment as if in thought, then continued. "How is it that you were on the Humphries estate, Randy? Were you supposed to be there for some reason?"

Randy squirmed a little. He was afraid he'd be asked that question, and figured he'd have to tell the truth. He wasn't about to lie to a priest.

"Well, no, not exactly. As a matter of fact, that's why I came to you. I knew I was trespassing, but something pretty awful happened last night, and I thought maybe I could help out by doing a little investigating. You won't tell anybody, will you?"

"Since you brought this to me with the intent of getting it back to its rightful owner, no. I will keep your secret. I won't punish you for trying to do what's right. But you are going to have to be more careful, Randy. The sheriff called me about an hour ago and told me about the deer that was killed last night. I assume that's what you're referring to. A wild predator is nothing to fool around about. I'd just as soon not be doing your funeral any time soon. All right?"

"All right. Can you tell me what the medallion is, though?"

"Certainly, it's a medallion of St. Michael, the Archangel, who chased Lucifer and the rebellious angels out of heaven, and now guards it."

"Lucifer. You mean the devil?"

"Yes, Lucifer felt he had become more than the God that created him. He convinced many of the angels to join him in his rebellion. They were consequently thrown out of heaven."

"This morning, I saw an old Spanish map of this valley over at Fred's, I mean the sheriff's, that called it the Lair of the Devil. Do you really think the devil still exists in the modern world?"

"The devil is immortal. He's not going to cease to exist just because man has invented technologies that make him feel like he's mastering the universe. You only have to look at the world around you to see evidence of Satan. Sin originates from the devil, and it's certainly easy enough to find sin in the world."

Randy became uncomfortable talking about the devil. He shifted his feet back and forth nervously, and found his hands growing cold. He didn't know why, but he just felt a resurgence of the feeling of foreboding he had been dealing with most of the day.

"I hope Mr. Humphries will be happy to get his medallion back." Randy hoped to change the subject.

"I'm sure he will. Most of you kids just saw him as a grumpy old man that was always chasing you off of his property. In reality, he was a very sensitive, devout individual, deeply committed to his faith. He attended daily Mass every morning, and filled a small bottle of holy water that he took home with him."

Father Brian was interrupted by Thunder, who eased over to him and put his nose in Father's hand.

"I'm sorry I ignored you, Thunder." Father Brian knelt down to pet the dog more thoroughly. "I'm sure you realize that Saints are always welcome at my church."

"Thanks for your help, Father, but I'd better be getting home. It's almost dinner time, and I'm getting pretty hungry."

"Kids your age are always hungry. Go on home and have a good dinner. And feel free to stop by any time. I always enjoy talking to you."

Randy hurried off back home, still feeling chilly in spite of the bright sun shining overhead.

Chapter Five - Dinner

Randy went home, but instead of cutting through the estate, he took the long way around as he was supposed to. After finding out that dinner wasn't ready yet, he went to his room, fell onto his bed, and just stared at the ceiling, lost in thought. Randy had never been particularly fearful or easily frightened, yet he definitely felt on edge, and he couldn't figure out why. Since his parents did not avidly attend church, he had not given the subject of religion a great deal of thought. He knew his parents believed in God simply because they had told him; but there again, this belief had never been a major topic of discussion. They attended church each Easter and Christmas, and always said grace before dinner. That aspect of his life had always been so routine that he never questioned it. But now he wondered. Randy found himself wishing that his parents had talked more about their beliefs, so that he would have something to fall back on. Did he really believe in his heart of hearts that God existed? He wasn't sure. For some reason the possibility of the devil existing seemed much more believable. But that didn't make sense either. He realized you couldn't believe in one and not the other. If the devil existed, then God had to exist.

He figured he'd worry about his beliefs later. The fact was, something dangerous was on the loose. He had complete confidence in Fred to handle the situation, and he knew he'd promised to do nothing until Fred got back, but he'd already sort of broken that promise. At this point, he might as well do a little more investigating. That way when Fred did get back they could combine all their information and have more to go on. Even Fred would be able to see the logic of that. He decided that tomorrow morning he'd check out the Humphries' mansion since that seemed to be the origin of the prints.

He heard his dad come home and decided to tackle him for information about the Humphries' place. Randy went to the family room to wait for his dad there. His dad had been working on rewiring the theater system to try to make it easier to operate. Randy couldn't understand the problem. He found the system easy enough to work with. Why mom was always complaining that she couldn't figure it out, was beyond him.

"Randy, I'm glad you're here to help me. It always makes it easier to have a second person to help pull wires through and hand you things. We won't have a lot of time to work on it tonight though. Your mom is already busy with dinner, and it should be ready soon." Jake stepped in behind the equipment.

Some years ago Jake had gutted the twenty by thirty-foot family room to put the theater system in, and was always tinkering with it, trying to make improvements. The massive bass speaker was built into the wall behind the screen and main speakers. The subwoofer covered half of the twenty-foot wall. There were seven, seven-foot tall columns about eight inches square that served as main speakers. Three across the front (left, center, right), one on each side, and two to the rear. There was a stack of amplifiers almost five feet tall powering the speakers. Everyone, including Fred and Ellen, thought Jake was giving in to overkill, but Jake was happy. Ellen was willing to put up with the house shaking from time to time if Jake was content. Since there were only two small narrow windows on one of the side walls, the room was naturally dark to begin with. This helped control light when the ceiling mounted projector was turned on and the screen dropped in front of the center speaker. The equipment was mounted on the other side wall in a large cabinet that swung out for easy access.

"Randy. Got a call from Fred at the office. Said there might be some predator prowling around the valley that could be dangerous. Told me you could fill me in on the details. What's up? Say, hand me those cables on the chair, would you?"

Randy handed the cables to his dad and briefly told him about the animal tracks outside the window, and his find in the woods.

"Well, you'd better be careful. Hopefully, whatever is out there is nocturnal and won't bother us during the day. Even so, stay out of the woods. And if for any reason you do have to go somewhere, take Thunder with you. He's a lot fiercer than he looks, and as close as the two of you are, I'm sure he'd do anything to protect you."

"Dad, where's Thunder going to sleep at night? I know that Rachel is scared of him, but we can't leave him outside with some creature prowling around."

"Good question, Randy. Let's discuss it with your mom at dinner, which I would guess, should be ready by now. Let's go eat."

They washed up and headed to the dining room. The table was ready to go when they got there, and Ellen and Rachel were just getting seated. Jake and Randy quickly took their places. The table was covered with large bowls of mashed potatoes, gravy, corn, rolls, and a platter of fried chicken. Since they usually ate in the kitchen, Randy assumed they were having dinner in the dining room for Rachel's benefit. The dining room was far more formal looking, with the lacquered walnut furniture gleaming in the candlelight. Randy disliked eating there, however. He was always afraid he would spill something on the white tablecloth.

"Let's join hands and say grace," Jake said for Rachel's benefit.

Randy couldn't help but notice that Rachel paled somewhat at his father's suggestion, and with eyes closed and head bowed, she trembled slightly during the short prayer. When she raised her head, there seemed to be a smoldering in her eyes, as though she were having trouble controlling intense emotion.

"Mom, where's Thunder going to sleep, now that there's some wild animal roaming around the valley?"

"Randy, what are you talking about? What wild animal?"

"Oh, you haven't heard?" Jake was trying to talk in-between mouthfuls. "Fred put out the word this afternoon that a dead deer had been found in the valley, pretty badly mauled up. He's concerned there may be a large predator on the loose. He was going to take the body into the city to see if anyone would have an idea as to what killed it. In the meantime, he suggested that we all be a little more careful until he gets back, especially at night."

"What kind of danger are we in?" Ellen stopped eating out of obvious concern. Ellen did not particularly enjoy this aspect of mountain living. She was very gentle by nature and did not like the prospect of anyone or anything being harmed.

"Very little, if any. Most large predators hunt at night, so as long as everyone stays indoors after dark we'll be just fine. We should also keep Thunder indoors at night until this is resolved."

"He won't be able to come to my room and scare me will he?" Rachel paled somewhat at the mention of Thunder.

"No," reassured Jake. "Randy can keep him in his room at night and take him back outside in the morning. That reminds me, however. Your dad called me at the office this morning and apologized for just leaving you on our doorstep. Said he got a call from his in-laws in the wee hours of the morning, that one of Becky's sisters had had a heart attack and ended up in the coronary care section of the hospital. Rachel wouldn't be allowed in intensive care, and since the hospital is in Nebraska, they wanted to leave right away. Uncle Bill said he did call us first, and that *you* answered the phone, Randy. Why didn't you tell us? And what were you doing answering the phone at five in the morning?" He reached across the table for another helping of mashed potatoes.

"I don't know what you're talking about, honest. I didn't answer any telephone this morning."

"Well, Bill and I might not be very close, but he's always been honest to a fault. And as protective as he is about Rachel, I can't imagine him not calling first. Are you into answering the phone in your sleep now?"

"Dad, I don't remember the phone ringing, *honest!*" Randy looked his father in the eyes with genuine perplexity.

"Well, I don't know. I have to admit, I don't remember the phone ringing early this morning myself. When Bill and Becky get back, we'll see if they can shed some more light on this. In the meantime, Rachel, are you doing all right? You've been awfully quiet since you've been here."

"I'm okay, Uncle Jake." Rachel slouched down in her chair.

"What happened to your finger? It's all bandaged up."

"I hurt it on the front porch this morning, Uncle Jake. It feels much better now that Aunt Ellen took care of it for me."

"The poor dear didn't even tell me she had gotten hurt this morning." Ellen was busy handing Rachel the butter dish. "It wasn't until we were ready to go shopping that I noticed she had torn the finger nail off. She was a very brave girl to hold so still while I washed and dressed it. She didn't even cry."

They fell silent, everyone paying attention to dinner. As always, Randy packed away an enormous quantity of food, and wolfed everything down as if he were starving. Randy was the first one to finish with the main course and reach for the cherry pie that was waiting for dessert.

"Randy, what did you do this afternoon?" Ellen was eating slowly so she could avoid desert. She hoped to lose a few pounds. "We missed you at the park."

"I'm sorry I didn't come over and join you Mom, but I was still a little shook up at finding that deer this morning."

Ellen dropped her fork on her plate and swung around to face Randy. "*You're* the one who found the deer? Why didn't someone tell me *you* found it?"

"You didn't ask." Jake kicked himself in the leg as soon as he said it. "Hon, I'm sorry." He saw Ellen's face cloud up. "But you're sometimes over-protective of Randy, and he's got to be allowed a little freedom. He and the other kids in town always go exploring around the valley, and once in a great while they're likely to come across the remains of some predator's supper. A supper that was caught, killed, and eaten during the night, when the kids are safe in their beds."

"Our son could have been that supper!" Ellen's face had become flushed. She turned back to Randy. "And what else were you doing today that I haven't heard about?"

"Thunder and I took a little walk, and ran into Father Brian at the church. He was working on his garden, and I spent a little time talking to him."

Randy might have imagined it, but he thought for sure that at the mention of Father Brian's name, that Rachel looked briefly his way with a startled look in her blue eyes.

"Did you talk about anything in particular?" Jake hoped to steer the conversation away from the deer.

"No. I asked him if he really thought the devil still existed in today's modern world, and he said yes. You only had to look at all the sin in the world."

"The devil," remarked Jake. "What prompted you to bring that up?"

"Well, when I was at Fred's this morning, after showing him where that deer was, I saw this old map that he had found. It labeled this valley as the Lair of the Devil. It sort of got me thinking."

"I'm beginning to wonder who in town hasn't seen that map." Jake put his fork down and raised his hands in exasperation. "Fred showed it to me last week. I tried to convince him to keep it under his hat. If everyone starts calling this place the Lair of the Devil, we'll have lots of properties for sale, but no buyers."

This time Randy was certain he had not imagined it. At the mention of the devil and the map, Rachel looked up at him and stared right into his eyes. What chilled him was that the stare was not what he expected from a small child. He found himself drawn deeply into her eyes. With an effort of will, he turned his head away from her.

The rest of dinner was occupied with Jake bringing Ellen up to date with the day's real estate happenings. Randy was more than happy to finish his dessert in silence, and be excused to his room. He was still going over the day's events in his mind, when his father brought Thunder to him and reminded him to keep the dog there until morning, and keep the door closed.

Chapter Six - Noises in the Night

In the middle of the night, the sound of Thunder growling woke Randy out of a deep sleep. Groggy, he raised up on his elbow to try to clear his head. Groaning, he swung his legs out of the bed and sat up. The dog was lying by the door, sniffing and then growling again.

"Hey buddy, what's wrong?" Randy got out of bed and went over to the dog. Thunder looked up and wagged his tail as Randy knelt next to him and scratched the top of his head.

"What's got you spooked?" The big dog whined and pawed at the door. "You know I can't let you out. If Rachel ran into you and got scared, I'd get in trouble with Mom and Dad. Won't you please go back to sleep?"

Thunder growled in response, and looked up at Randy.

"All right, I'll go out and take a look. But you stay here." Randy stood up and reached for the doorknob, and was surprised when the dog also stood up and blocked the way by leaning against the door.

"Thunder, I'll be fine. I'll stay in the house and I'll be right back," Randy gently pulled the dog away from the door.

Randy stepped silently into the hallway and looked around. The nightlight plugged into the wall outlet cast a warm but dim glow. Nothing appeared to be out of the ordinary, and he turned to go back into his room. A soft click and thud stopped him. It sounded like a door had been opened and closed at the back of the house. He crept down the hall to investigate. When he reached the doorway to the kitchen he peered in. Seeing nothing, he listened for further sounds. Holding his breath, he thought he heard very faint steps, as if some one were going into the basement. A sudden creak of the bottom step confirmed his suspicions. He opened the basement door, turning the knob as quietly as possible, and stared down into the darkness. He breathed as softly as he could.

A shiver went down his spine. The basement always scared him. Why, he couldn't explain, even to himself. He just couldn't shake the feeling that something down there was watching him.

He didn't know what to do. If he woke his parents, he'd get the... *you're just imagining things again... you're too old to be scared of the dark... go back to bed...* speech.

Taking a deep breath he started to tiptoe down the stairs into the inky darkness. His hand automatically reached for the light switch, and his fingers were about to throw the switch, when he stopped. It would alert whoever might be down there.

His palms began to sweat, making his hand slip along the handrail. The cool, moist basement air flowed up to meet him, making him shiver. Avoiding the bottom step, he made it down the stairs silently, and peered down the hall.

The basement was unfinished, and used primarily for storage. The hallway went straight back to a large room at the end, with three rooms coming off to the side. The first was the laundry room, the middle contained the utilities, and the third was storage. Jake and Randy had once tried to set up a model train layout in the large room at the end, but neither one had ever stuck with it. Jake always had too many projects going, and Randy felt the most uncomfortable in that room.

As Randy stared into the darkness, he saw a dim light that appeared to come from the room at the end. His fear took his breath away.

That was it, he'd had enough. He'd wake up his parents, regardless of what they'd tell him.

He tried to turn around, but couldn't. The dim light held his eyes, and he couldn't look away. He felt his will dissolve as the light flooded into his mind, eliminating all resistance. Horrified, he watched his feet begin to shuffle forward. His short, staccato breaths echoed in his ears. The rapid booming of his heart filled his chest.

The large stones that made up the floor felt cold and damp under his bare feet. The smell of laundry detergent filled the air. As he passed each of the doorways at his side, he felt a cold draft brush against him. Each time, he felt as though something would reach out of the blackness and grab him. Whooosh, the hot water heater turned on, and Randy jumped in spite of the light's control.

By the time he got to the end, tears were flowing down his cheeks. He was shaking as he tried to stop from going into the room. He wanted to close his eyes, block out the light, but couldn't. Through the fog that wrapped around his mind, he thought he heard heavy footsteps come up from behind, and heard his name being called out.

The light vanished. The stone floor shuddered ever so slightly as he heard a soft but powerful thud. His mind clear again, he reached over to turn on the light. He blinked as his eyes adjusted to the bright light flooding the room. Something touched Randy's shoulder, and he screamed. Looking down, he saw a hand settle by his neck. He spun around to see his father standing in the hallway, obviously startled at Randy's reaction.

"I didn't mean to scare you, son. I got up to use the bathroom and thought I heard a noise in the basement. I figured I'd check it out. Are you okay?"

Randy threw his arms around his father. "Thunder woke me up by growling at the door. I thought I heard someone go into the basement. I didn't want to wake you guys up, so I came down here myself. After that, I don't know what happened. I'm just so scared." He tightened his grip around his father.

Jake patted his son on the back. "It's okay, take it easy. Let's see what we can find."

Randy felt his arms being gently pulled away, and let his father lead him into the room.

The room was twenty feet by thirty feet with two large posts in the center. Off to one side was the large train layout. As with everything else in the room - - boxes, old lamps, stacked cans of paint - - it was covered with a thick layer of dust. Cobwebs hung from the ceiling, stretching down to some of the mountains in the layout. The swaying of two bare light bulbs on their cords cast very defined shadows that rocked back and forth.

"We've got to clean this place up, Randy. Hey, look at the floor. The dust on the floor seems to be smudged in a path from the hall over to the far wall."

Randy saw the trail through the dust and followed his father. The trail led to a small opening right at the floor that was about six inches in diameter. The wall was made up of odd shaped stones that were fitted together like a giant jigsaw puzzle. Jake squatted down and picked up a rock that was lying just to the side of the opening.

"Well, this is what used to be in that hole. It looks like we probably have rats in our basement. I'll bet that's what you heard." Jake held his hand in front of the opening. "Randy, check out the draft coming out of this hole."

Randy reached down and was amazed at the strong current of air that rushed though his fingers.

Jake stood, placed his hands on his hips, and arched his back. "You know, there're rumors that there's supposed to be a network of caves running throughout this valley, left by the miners that used to work the area. How much do you want to bet that somewhere this hole connects into some cave?

"I'll have to get some exterminators in here to kill off the rats, and then we'll have to cement up that hole. Please don't tell your mother about this. She's terrified of mice and rats. If she thought there was even the slimmest possibility of coming across either one down here, we'd probably end up doing our own laundry for the rest of our lives. Either that, or I'd end up having to build another laundry room on the main floor. And since I don't feel like doing either, mums the word. All right?"

"Whatever you say." Randy had calmed down, and thought this might be a good time to find out more about the Humphries' house. "Dad, what about the old Humphries' place? Isn't it strange that I first saw those animal prints outside the broken window of the place, then the next day they show up outside our house, then later with that mauled deer?"

"I don't know what to tell you, Randy. I admit I didn't get a chance to check out the broken window today, and probably won't tomorrow either, as busy as things have been at the office. I'm having to fill in for your mother also. I went through the entire house myself just last week, and I assure you, there were no wild animals trapped in the place. Granted, the house has sort of a creepy feel to it. But I think that's to be expected. When you walk through it you can't help but think about the murder that took place there years ago."

Jake reached down to wipe some dust off his robe where it had brushed up against the wall. "The place is real drafty, and there is supposed to be a network of secret passageways and stairways throughout the entire mansion. I have to admit, I have a hard time believing that. I've been through the place several times now, and it's mostly built out of solid stone. It would take some real ingenious architecture to design hidden doorways into stone walls, and make them movable. But I tell you what. As soon as things settle down at the office, I'll take you on a tour of the place, how's that? In the meantime, let's get back to bed."

Jake led the way back down the hallway and up the stairs. He turned the corner at the top of the stairs and went into the back entrance of the master bedroom suite. Randy continued onward to his own bedroom. As he passed Rachel's room, he noticed that the door was open a few inches, and that there was a light turned on in the room. Curious, he pushed the door open a little wider, and quietly stuck his head in to look around. There was a night light on next to the bed, but no Rachel.

"Rachel," he called out softly. "Are you all right?"

There was no answer. He went into the room and looked around. There was no sign of her. Randy noticed a picture on the nightstand next to the bed, and picked it up. It was a school picture of Rachel. Randy remembered his parents receiving one like it just a few months ago. He checked the closet, but only found her clothes hanging there. He was about to go wake his parents, when he turned around and found

Rachel standing in the doorway. She was wearing a pink nightgown, her bare feet poking out from underneath.

"Rachel, where were you? I was coming down the hallway, and found your door open. Are you okay?"

"I wasn't feeling well and had to go to the bathroom. I feel better now. Thanks, Randy."

"No problem, cuz. I'll just head back to bed. Hope you sleep all right."

Randy headed out of the room, and Rachel closed the door behind him. Just as the door was almost closed, he happened to glance down. His eyes went wide with astonishment as he thought he saw two sets of dusty footprints on the dark blue rug in Rachel's room. One set was his own, since he had forgotten to wipe his feet after walking in the basement, but the other was much smaller and more delicate. He only saw them for an instant, but was sure that he was not imagining things. He looked down at the hallway floor, but couldn't see anything on the gray carpeting.

Shaking, and not knowing what to think, he went back to his room. Thunder was relieved to see him, and he gave the dog a big hug. He felt so tired and shook up, that he just fell into bed. He decided he'd sort it all out in the morning. As he fell asleep, the moon broke through the cloud cover and filled the room with a pale glow. Thunder kicked his feet and growled in his sleep.

Chapter Seven - The Humphries House

Randy woke early the next morning to find Thunder licking his face. It took him awhile to drag himself out of bed and let Thunder outside, but he forced himself regardless. Cleaning up the mess made by a St. Bernard who absolutely had to go to the bathroom was not a pleasant task.

He had not slept well. Even though he went back to bed super tired, his sleep had been fitful, filled with half forgotten shadows and terrors. He woke with the sound of mocking laughter echoing in his head. After getting dressed, he went by Rachel's room to see about the footprints, but could find no sign of them.

Rachel was already at the breakfast table when he got there, and greeted him with a smug look that made him uneasy, especially coming from the face of a six-year-old. He wolfed down his breakfast and couldn't wait to get out of there.

After breakfast, Randy headed over to the Humphries' house. He just couldn't shake the feeling that it was the key to all the strange events of the past two days. He didn't tell his parents. He knew they would be furious.

He approached the broken window, deciding it would be the best way to get in. The massive mansion towered over him. Just overhead, there was a second story balcony that cast a deep shadow over the side of the house. He looked for the prints in the dirt, but all signs were washed away by the rain that fell during the night.

The latch was rusted and difficult to move, and he had to be careful not to cut his arms on the broken glass while he worked it loose. Sliding the window upwards, he slipped in the mud, and barely grabbed the window sill in time to keep from falling.

Once inside, he found himself in a large basement room. The floor and walls were made up of the same stones as the basement of his house. The room was empty of furniture, so he had no idea what it was once used for. It took a few moments for his eyes to adjust to the dim light, and he mentally kicked himself for not bringing a flashlight.

Being in a basement, he was surprised by the high ceilings and the fancy molding that ran along the top of the walls. He shook his head from side to side, deciding that they must have spent a lot of money when they built the house.

A large, arched opening led into a second room that was the same size, but did not have any doorways. Going back to the first room, he saw a large door in the center of the wall opposite the window, and went to it hoping it would lead into the house. The massive door creaked and moved slowly as Randy pulled with all his strength. The hallway beyond was dimly lit, and Randy had to walk carefully, his eyes were still adjusting to the darkness. He found that the stones making up the floor were much more evenly set than in his house. A great deal more care had been exercised in the building of the main house than the guesthouse.

Rather than trying to explore the basement, he was interested in checking out the upper floors first. He ignored the rooms that opened off the hallway, and went directly toward the stairs that he could barely see at the end. The stairs were broad, and surprisingly gentle in their ascent, not like the steep staircases so often found in modern homes. The door at the top of the stairs was open, and led into a hallway leading from the main entrance hall of the house. He walked as quietly as possible, not wanting to disturb the stillness of the house.

As he entered the main entrance hall, his breath was taken away by the size of it. The ceiling was three stories up, and the immense curved staircase led first to the second floor, then continued to the third. There were large arched entryways on either side of the hall that led to the living room on one side, and what must have been the library on the other.

He proceeded to the living room, and his attention was drawn to the enormous fireplace on the opposite wall. It was large enough for a grown man to stand up in, and wide enough to hold six foot logs. Natural stones, most of which were more than a foot in diameter, were intricately laid to make up the hearth and surrounding rockwork. Even so, the fireplace did not seem out of proportion to the room. The ceilings were at least twelve-foot high, and Randy guestimated the room to be thirty feet across, and forty feet long.

At the rear of the living room another arched opening led into the dining room. Almost as large as the living room itself, it must have been capable of hosting some large dinners. All the wood trim, doorways, and crown moldings were so ornately carved, that Randy could fully believe that it must have taken the ten years to build the house as was rumored.

He continued on through a door that led into the kitchen. Here again, a large fireplace, and a massive wood burning stove dominated the room. The place had never been modernized, except at the very end where a small efficiency appliance unit had been installed. Randy assumed old man Humphries had done it for his own personal use. Since the kitchen was built across the back of the house, several doors led out of it. One to the back porch, one to the hallway that led to the entrance hall, another that opened up into what must have been the servant's stairway to the upstairs, and yet another that led back around into the library.

He decided to follow around into the library, and wondered what it must have looked like with all of its shelves full. The library was also quite large, about thirty by forty-five feet, and lined floor to cciling with bookshelves all the way around. The only breaks in the shelving, were for the various doorways, and a fireplace on one wall that appeared to be identical to the one in the living room. The plaster crown molding was especially intricate, with delicate floral patterns winding their way around the top of the room. A stunning three-foot tall chandelier hung from the center of the ceiling.

Randy left to explore the upper floors. At the second floor landing, there was a double doorway on the immediate left, and a broad hallway that ran to the right. A narrow hallway led to the back of the house. All the doors were open, so it was easy to peer into the rooms to see what they were. The double doors led into the master bedroom suite, several times the size of his parent's bedroom. The suite had a separate sitting room with a fireplace, two separate walk-in closets with dressing rooms, and a bathroom that was as large as his entire bedroom. It must be nice to be able to live like this, he thought.

He went back to the hallway and followed the right branch first. There were seven large bedroom suites that came off it. Each had its own bathroom, large walk-in closet, and dressing room.

The hallway leading to the back of the house went to the servants quarters. There was a small two-bedroom apartment, with a separate stairway leading from the living room down to the kitchen.

Going up to the third floor, he found an enormous room that he thought must have been used as a ballroom. There was a stage at one end with a dance floor in front of it. There were also several large windows that enjoyed a beautiful view of the valley.

Randy couldn't say why, but for some reason he was drawn to the library. He sensed that there was more to it than met the eye. He decided to go back and take a closer look.

As he re-entered the library, he was again struck by the presence of the room. He couldn't explain his feeling, but he was certain that this room had been a major center for the house. He followed the bookshelves all the way around the room, occasionally pushing them to make certain they didn't move. He was about to walk past the fireplace, when he made a curious observation. Whereas the fireplace in the living room had been blackened by obvious use, this one was not. Like the rest of the house, the fireplace had been thoroughly cleaned, making it look like new. But even a thorough cleaning would not have removed fire-hardened soot from the walls. Randy stepped in to take a closer look. The stones that made up the fireplace were perfectly fitted, a testimonial to the craftsmanship that had gone into the house. He looked all around and up the chimney, but didn't see anything unusual. As he started to step out, he was surprised to feel a strong draft brush his cheek. He held his hand up to feel the airflow, and followed it to one of the sides. Here, even though the stones were still fitted perfectly together, there appeared to be faint gaps in the corners. As he moved his fingers along the seams, he could feel the air softly flowing through the corners. He continued to check the corners up and down with his fingertips. Just as he reached with his right hand up into the darkness, his hand slid into a crevice that had a handle in it. He grabbed it and gave a pull. He heard a loud click, and the entire wall moved ever so slightly. Excited, he put his shoulder to the wall and shoved. A cloud of stale and dusty air puffed out as the wall noiselessly swung open to reveal a narrow staircase leading downwards. The stairs vanished into the darkness, but he saw that just inside the opening was a small shelf with a candelabra on it and a book of matches.

    Shaking with excitement, he took the candelabra and lit the half-melted candles. With the flames wavering in the draft, he descended down the stairs. The musty atmosphere made breathing difficult. The narrow stone steps continued straight down for a considerable distance. By the time Randy reached the bottom, he was far below the basement of the house. He turned into a chamber once again lined with bookshelves, only this time they were filled with dusty books. In the center of the room was a small wooden table with a padded armchair set before it. As he raised the candelabra to take a better look at the books, he felt a chill go down his spine when he looked at the titles: *The Book of Spells and Incantations; The Black Mass; History of Voodooism; The Book of Forbidden Rituals; Basic Witchcraft.* They were all reference books concerning demonology, witchcraft, and the like. Randy left them alone. He had no desire to be the first to read their secrets after all these years. He wondered if this is where the infamous mistress of the house had done her studying of the occult. She had obviously acquired an enormous collection on the subject.

He saw a single large book on the table. His curiosity aroused, he bent down to take a closer look. With all the dust on the book, he couldn't make out the writing. He took a deep breath, and blew the dust away. It took awhile for the air to clear. When it did, he saw that it had "Diary" embossed on the cover. Carefully he opened it, the stiff pages crackling as they were turned. In a very delicate handwriting on the inside cover was written 'The Diary of Rachel Humphries.' He closed it back up again, feeling like he was violating someone's secrets. "Rachel," he said aloud, then became thoughtful as the echoes died down. Could it be more than just coincidence? No way, he thought. That would be too weird.

On the other side of the chamber, there was a massive wooden door that had been broken open. Randy took a closer look and saw that it was made out of solid wood two inches thick, hung on huge iron hinges that had been anchored into the rock. He decided that whatever had broken down that door was something he didn't want to meet. He started to step past the door when he came to an abrupt halt. He felt a sense of dread for whatever lay beyond that door, and couldn't quite muster the courage to keep going. Besides, he rationalized to himself, he didn't trust the candlelight. If they suddenly went out, he would find himself in utter darkness and would have problems finding his way back out.

On the opposite wall, there was an opening to a stairway that seemed to go back into the house. Since his intuition did not seem to be as negative there, he decided to check it out. It was narrow, and he had to turn sideways at times to get through. It went up a short distance before he came to a branch. Going up the left side first, he turned and twisted, and continued upwards some distance until he came to a panel. Looking up he saw a lever. Pulling it released the panel, which opened into one of the dressing rooms of the master bedroom. He checked the outside of the panel and discovered that one of the coat hooks could be pulled to open it from the outside.

Going back into the passageway, and following it back down, he took the other branch, and after going up an equal distance, found it emptied into an equally narrow hallway that was part of a network that went though the entire second floor. In each case, however, there was always a panel that opened into a dressing room. At least the designer was consistent in his method of concealment. The only parts of the house that didn't seem to have any secret passageways were the basement and third floor.

By the time he was through exploring, he had a pretty good feel for the house and how it was constructed. He did start to wonder, however, if *his* house had any similar passageways, or if somehow the two houses might be connected in some fashion. Since he had no intention of exploring the other corridor without better lighting, he decided to go back home and see if he could use some of what he had learned to find anything.

When he got home, he found a note on the kitchen table from his mother, explaining that she had left to run errands, and taken Rachel with her. Randy decided this was a perfect opportunity to snoop around without raising any questions. Remembering the draft coming out of the rat hole he and his father had discovered the night before, he decided to start his search there. First, he got his flashlight from his room. He had no desire to be exploring in the dark again. Since Rachel was not in the house, he took Thunder down to the basement with him. He always felt more secure down there with the big dog.

Since all the trigger mechanisms had been higher up in the main house, he carefully inspected all the rocks along the top of the wall to see if any were loose. He was soon rewarded by finding one that pulled out. He reached in and could barely control his excitement when he felt a handle in it. When he gave a tug, he could hear the same click he had heard in the library fireplace back in the mansion. He put his shoulder against the wall, and pushing hard, saw a section of the wall slowly glide backwards until there was enough clearance on either side to walk around it. Shining his flashlight upwards, he saw that the section of wall hung from two large tracks that allowed it to slide back and forth. He assumed that one would have to grasp the handle in the top hole to pull it shut.

He felt the same sense of dread that he experienced at the broken door in the main house's underground chamber, but with Thunder with him to help calm his nerves, he felt he could go on. He called Thunder, and was surprised that the dog stopped in the opening and started to growl.

"Oh, come on Thunder, don't tell me you're afraid of the dark. Will you please come with me."

Thunder had a look of uncertainty in his eyes, but he wasn't about to let Randy go by himself. Randy stepped around the door and shone his flashlight into the chamber. He found a stone passageway six feet wide and eight feet tall that headed off in the general direction of the main house. With Thunder at his side, he crept carefully along, shining his flashlight at the walls as he went. He had gone about thirty feet when he came to a fork. He shone his flashlight first one way then another. The left side was a continuation of the stone passageway, while the right appeared to be a natural cave. He started to go up the right hand side, but was promptly stopped by Thunder who grabbed his hand and started growling. Randy had felt an uneasiness come over him as he tried to go in that direction, so he was only too willing to agree, and took the left hand passage instead. He followed along for what seemed forever, when he stepped into a larger cavern. On one side was the broken door that led into the sub-chamber under the mansion. On the other side, a steel cage had been constructed and anchored into the solid rock. It was very large, at least twenty feet square, with the cave wall serving as the back of the enclosure. What seemed so out of place, was the furniture.

A four-post bed had been placed on one side. An oak dining table with a single chair was in the center, and a roll-top oak desk was on the other side with a chest of drawers next to it. The steel door to the cage was still closed, but the bars had been bent apart. Stepping inside, Randy saw a picture on the desk. He picked it up, and saw that it was a picture of a blond woman, in her mid-forties, with blue eyes. Turning it over he saw that it was labeled "Rachel Humphries." Randy couldn't help but notice the similarity in features between the woman in the picture, and his cousin Rachel. They both had the same high forehead, and sharply defined cheekbones. A chill went through him, when he noticed that the blue eyes, in particular, seemed so similar. Putting it down, he continued to glance about the cage. He took in a sharp breath when he saw that in some soft dirt along one of the cave walls, were the same animal tracks that he had been trying to locate for the past couple of days.

Now he was faced with a dilemma. If he told his parents, he would be in more trouble than he cared to be for going into the Humphries' house. But, if he said nothing, wasn't he placing everyone in danger? And then there was Rachel. He couldn't figure her out at all. Since he had known his cousin long before all this happened, he didn't see how she could be involved. And yet he just wasn't sure. Well, Fred had planned to be back this afternoon, so he decided he'd confess everything to him. Fred would be angry, but would forgive him more quickly.

Becoming frightened, he made his way back to his own house with Thunder at his side. As he went down the passageway, however, he began to get more and more terrified, as if something was following them. He lost his composure, and yelling for Thunder, started to run. Side by side, they sped back home, with the feeling of dread catching up. Randy's breath came in big gasps, as terror seemed to slowly engulf him from behind. As they came to the wall in front of the basement opening, Thunder went around to the right, but just as Randy started around to the left, something caught him from behind, and pulled him back. He began to scream when he received a sharp blow on the side of his head and passed out.

   Thunder, realizing that something was wrong, skidded to a stop and started back to the wall. Just as he got there, it pushed shut in his face, and separated him from Randy. At first he just sniffed, but after a while, began to howl and bark at the stone wall.

Chapter Eight - Janet

After Randy left Fred's house, Fred drove back up to the meadow. He put the remains of the deer in a plastic body bag, and loaded them into the Jeep. Since it was already mid-afternoon, and a good two-hour drive into Mesa Springs, he decided he would spend the night there and not get back until the next day. He left warnings of caution at the key gathering places in town: the post office, the grocery store, and so on. He knew it wouldn't take long for the word to spread.

He was concerned about Randy staying out of trouble until he got back. Randy had a tendency to be somewhat impetuous, and sometimes threw caution aside when his determination kicked in. Fred wondered if maybe he should have talked to Jake in more detail before he left. Oh well, it was too late now. Besides, what trouble could Randy possibly get into in only twenty-four hours?

Fred spent the drive into the city listening to music and enjoying the scenery. Even though he would have saved a little time by taking the interstate, the back roads were more scenic and not so heavily traveled. There would be plenty of opportunities to deal with heavy traffic in the city.

Mesa Springs was not large, having a population of only 500,000. Its location, however, helped to make it a hub for the surrounding area. It was nestled at the base of the foothills, and was a more attractive place to live than the oversized state capitol some 100 miles out on the plains where it was not only much hotter, but lacked the natural beauty of the adjacent mountains.

His first destination was the university. He made many friends while in attendance, and maintained those friendships over the subsequent years. One such friend was Janet. He and Janet met as fellow students, and developed a close relationship during their years together at the university. Even though there had been talk of marriage, they seemed to drift apart after graduation. Janet elected to stay at the university and pursue her post graduate studies, and eventually her doctorate degree in zoology. She just couldn't seem to separate herself from her research. Over time the relationship cooled down, and they each pursued their own separate paths.

The ride into Mesa Springs was uneventful, and Fred soon found himself enjoying the nostalgia of the familiar sights of the campus. Established over a hundred years ago, the grounds enjoyed the shade of mature trees overhanging the paths and roadways. Fred couldn't help but notice a group of very attractive female students chatting by one of the park benches. He wished that he were twenty years younger again.

He pulled into a parking space in front of the animal sciences building. He did not talk to Janet personally when he called before he left, but instead verified with an assistant of hers that she would be in today, and what her office hours were. He felt somewhat uneasy as he walked into the open door of her office. He would not admit it, even to himself, but Janet still occupied a very special place in his heart. She had been his first serious love, and he never got over his feelings for her.

Fred stepped into her office and looked around. As is usually the case with university offices, this one was extremely small with barely enough room for the gray metal desk and file cabinet. Janet looked just as Fred remembered her, tall and slender, with a youthful appearance that had made the two of them such a handsome couple. Her black hair gently draped about her shoulders, providing an interesting contrast to her light hazel eyes.

Janet looked up as Fred stepped over to her desk. She let out a small gasp of surprise as genuine pleasure lit up her face. "You still like to catch people off guard and surprise them don't you. Of all the people I expected to see today, you've got to be last on the list. How many years has it been?" She stood up and gave Fred a warm embrace.

"Too many. I'd forgotten how beautiful you are, and just had to refresh my memory."

"Right, you bet." Janet left her arms on Fred's shoulders and looked into his eyes. "What do you want, Fred? You know, I never could turn you down."

"Well, I've got a small problem I was hoping you could help me with. A deer was killed, up above town, and pretty badly mauled in the process. We don't get many predators that close to town, and I was hoping you could take a look at the remains and give me an idea of what we're dealing with."

"Sure, let's head over to the lab. Grab a cart to wheel it in on, and we'll take a look."

Janet led the way down the hall to the lab. Her white lab coat did not do justice to her figure, but Fred didn't care. His memories of her were so vivid that she could have worn a barrel as far as he was concerned.

She made a production of grabbing Fred's left hand, and raising it up to look at it. "Not remarried yet? Haven't found some sweet young thing to conquer your heart yet?" Janet teased.

"You're the only one who managed to completely conquer my heart, Janet."

"A flirt as always. Just be careful. Some day I might expect you to follow through."

The cart certainly made the job of getting the deer into the lab a lot easier. Even so, they both strained to get the heavy carcass out of the Jeep, and were winded by the time they managed to push the heavy load into the lab.

The lab had the antiseptic look of a hospital operating room, with shiny white tiles covering the floor, walls, and ceiling. There were several large cabinets around the perimeter of the room, all with bottles and medical supplies visible behind their glass doors. There were four examining tables in the room, and Janet steered the cart to the closest one.

"I'm glad to see that my presence still makes you breathe heavy," Fred quipped as he stretched his back to relieve the sore muscles.

"Still indulging in wishful thinking, I see." Janet unzipped the body bag.

Fred decided he was not coming out on top with his attempts at verbal volleyball, and decided to keep his peace for awhile. Not only that, but the sight of the bag's contents had a sobering effect.

Janet checked the deer's wounds, and frowned as she studied them more closely. When she noticed the opened chest cavity, and the missing heart, she turned to Fred with a perplexed look on her face.

"Are you sure this isn't the work of some cult? No animal alive could have inflicted these wounds, much less have removed the heart. Look at these deep slashes. Instead of the ragged edges you'd see if they were made by an animal's claws, they're perfectly smooth, as if they were made by a razor sharp knife. Also, the carcass itself wasn't eaten from. The only part missing is the heart."

"The area where the deer was killed was surrounded by soft dirt. No one could have approached the area without leaving tracks. Which reminds me, I've got something else in the Jeep you should look at. Let me get it."

Fred returned a moment later carrying a box, which he set down by the remains. "Here are some plaster casts I made of the predator's prints. Maybe they'll help."

Janet removed them and took a close look. "Whatever made these certainly could have killed the deer. Notice how sharp and well defined the claw impressions are." She studied them more closely, and took some measurements. Her brow furrowed more. "I can't begin to tell you what made these tracks, however. I've never seen anything like them. The symmetry of the pads is more human-like than animal. I thought I was familiar with all the indigenous life in this area."

Janet was thoughtful for awhile. "Fred, what's going on. No animal on the face of this earth would kill just so it could remove its victim's heart, nor would it have the skill or intelligence to do it the way it was done here. Also, these castings don't look like anything I've ever seen. If this is your idea of a practical joke, I'm not amused."

"I wish it were a practical joke. If I had any answers, I wouldn't be here asking you for help."

"I tell you what, we've got a store room in back where we've got castings of every animal we've ever come across in these mountains. Some of them date back a hundred years or so. Let's go take a look at what's back there."

Janet washed up and led the way down the hall to the storeroom. The room had a musty odor, and was filled with rows of shelves piled up with dusty items of all descriptions. Everything from lifelike birds, mounted on pedestals, to shelves of bones. Along the back wall were the shelves of castings that Janet had spoken about. They commenced their search in silence, starting on opposite ends of the wall. There were literally hundreds of castings, and after spending what seemed like hours, Fred was about to suggest calling it quits when he spied one that looked a lot like his. "Janet, what's this?"

Janet came over and studied it more closely. "It sure looks identical to the one you brought. Let's see what the tag says. 'Casting of print found at scene of murder investigation at Humphries' estate, Shady Valley - unidentifiable.' Well, you're the sheriff up there, you tell me what this is all about."

Fred felt a chill go down his spine when Janet read the tag. He found himself worrying if Randy was all right. "The murder at the Humphries' place happened long before my time, fifty years ago. Since it was so sensational at the time, I've gone through the file, but there isn't much there. My predecessor, Harry, who was the sheriff at the time, obviously thought that Humphries wife had committed the murder as part of some satanic ritual, but he was never able to prove anything, so the case remained unsolved."

"Well the answer is obvious," laughed Janet. "The casting is from a demon summoned by Humphries' wife." Her laughter stopped short when she noticed the ashen look on Fred's face. "I'm sorry. You know I don't believe in nonsense like that. I didn't think you did either. I was just trying to lighten the mood."

"I don't know what to believe right now. But I think I had better look up old Harry. He moved down here to the city when he retired, and I brought his address with me just in case I needed it."

Fred was surprised when Janet threw her slender arms around him and gave him a tender kiss. She continued to hug him while resting her head on his shoulder.

"Be careful, please. Even though I don't believe in any spiritual nonsense, for some reason this whole thing scares me, and you know I don't scare easily. You may not know it, but you're still very special to me."

They continued to linger in each other's embrace before sharing one last kiss between the shelves of claws and paw prints.

Chapter Nine - The Lair of the Devil

Fred was in emotional disarray as he drove off the campus in search of a place for dinner. Janet turned down his invitation to join him, explaining she had classes to teach that evening, and still needed to prepare. She did, however, accept his offer of breakfast the next morning. Fred was happy to have some time to sort out his thoughts. Janet's kiss and revelation of her feelings had shaken him up, and he wasn't quite sure how to react. Their relationship during college had started out as a close, platonic friendship, and remained that way for the first couple of years. When they realized that their feelings had deepened, the transition to something more romantic had been awkward for both of them. Then with graduation upon them, the pressures of graduate school for Janet, and the challenge of starting a career for Fred, the transition had never been fully realized. Fred now found himself wondering about their break-up. Maybe their difficulty in finding time to get together had merely been an avoidance of dealing with their lack of maturity to form a solid relationship based on friendship, love, and intimacy. One of the things Fred had learned from his first marriage was that your mate not only had to be your lover, but your best friend as well. The headiness of being in love fades over time, and if the basis for a solid friendship doesn't exist, the love also fades away.

Fred pulled into the parking lot of a small restaurant that he used to frequent as a student. As he walked towards the door, he was surprised to see Jake's brother, Bill, come walking out with his wife Becky, and their daughter Rachel. In complete contrast to Jake, Bill was short and slender, and possessed a full head of dark brown hair. Jake and Bill always had trouble convincing people that they were brothers. Becky, on the other hand, was large for a woman, at just under six feet tall and over 200 pounds in weight. She prided herself on her waist length blond hair.

"Bill, a small world, isn't it. It seems I never see you in Shady Valley, even though it's only twenty miles from your place. But 100 miles away, I run into you in a restaurant parking lot. What brings you down to the city."

"We're starting out on a short vacation, and stopped here for dinner. Decided it was time to get away for awhile and unwind. How's that brother of mine been behaving? Still fooling around with his stereo all the time."

"You know Jake, he loves his toys. I have to admit though, I am somewhat confused. I thought for sure I heard Randy mention that Rachel was staying with them for a few days."

"I don't know what to tell you Fred. Rachel's been with us and hasn't spent the night anywhere else for months now. Besides, you know how shy she is. She rarely wants to be with anyone but us."

"Well, things have been a little wild in the valley. I probably confused someone else's story with Randy's. Have a great vacation!"

After dinner, Fred decided to drop in on Harry to see if he could shed any light on those paw prints, and their connection to the Humphries' investigation. He realized he probably should have called first, but decided he'd take a chance and see if he'd be lucky enough to catch Harry at home.

His luck held, and he was rewarded by seeing Harry's ever-smiling face when the door opened. Harry had aged considerably since Fred had last seen him. The sparse hair on his head had turned white. He also lost some height, and was no longer six feet tall like he used to be. Deep wrinkles covered his face and forehead, but his bright brown eyes still twinkled out from behind bushy eyebrows. Harry was someone who always found the silver lining to every cloud. If he couldn't find something to laugh about, then the situation was grim indeed.

"Fred, what tore you away from the valley?" Harry took Fred's hand and shook it vigorously. "If you drove all this way just to visit an old man in his retirement, I'm flattered. Come on in. Make yourself comfortable."

Harry led the way into the living room, and with a sweep of his arm, invited Fred to sit wherever he wished. Harry settled in a large, overstuffed chair by the fireplace. Fred looked around and concluded that Harry's finances had not fared well during his retirement. All the furniture sagged and was badly torn. There were several large holes in the dark brown carpeting. The cream colored paint covering the walls was peeling in several places, showing the bare plaster underneath. Even so, the place was clean. Fred saw no dust anywhere, and the large picture window looking out on the street glittered in the moonlight.

"Can I get you anything to drink or eat," offered Harry.

"No thanks, Harry. I just had dinner. And I wish I could say that this visit was just social, but I'm running into a problem in the valley that I hope you can shed some light on. I'm totally stumped."

"It's nice to know that even in our senility, us old folks still have some wisdom to share," laughed Harry. "How can I help?"

"Well," answered Fred, settling into his chair, "it appears we've got some predator loose in the valley that no one can recognize. Yesterday we found a deer up above the town, pretty badly torn up. Since I couldn't tell what did it, I took the remains of the deer and some castings of the predator's prints over to the university so a friend of mine there could take a look at them. Unfortunately, she couldn't figure out what made the kill either, or what could have made those prints. The only clue we could find was some castings of identical prints that were sitting in the storeroom collecting dust. They were tagged as having been found at the scene of the murder investigation at the Humphries' estate. I was hoping maybe you could help solve this mystery."

As he heard Fred's story, the smile began to fade from Harry's face. "Can you tell me what the deer's corpse looked like?" Harry got up to pour himself a drink at the bar by the fireplace.

"That's the strange part. It was almost completely shredded up, but no part of it seemed to have been consumed. The only part missing was its heart. And that seemed to be removed with surgical precision. Janet, my friend at the university, suggested that maybe a cult of some sort might be responsible."

"I wish you were that lucky. What do you know about the Humphries affair?"

"Not much. The file is curiously empty of any hard evidence. Just some basic facts of who the victim was, when the murder was committed, and so on. There's no autopsy report, or notes from any interviews with the Humphries themselves. There is one piece of evidence that piqued my curiosity, however. There was an old map in the file, obviously of the valley. It was hand written in Spanish, and labeled *Lair of the Devil*. It showed a network of caves in the valley, with the entrance somewhere in the town."

Harry's face paled somewhat at the mention of the map. All the joviality had been drained from it. "I hoped this day would never come, but somehow I always knew it would. The map you found in the file was part of a manuscript that I found at the Humphries' estate. Since it was blood stained, I thought it might be tied to the murder, and collected it as evidence. After I had it translated, and read the contents . . . well, maybe I'd better let you make your own judgment. Let me get it."

Harry returned carrying a large, leather-bound book that he treated with the utmost care. He sat back down in his chair and opened it in his lap. "It had been translated so that the English pages are inserted, in order, in the manuscript. I've read it so many times, I know most of it by heart. It's a diary written by one of the Spanish explorers of the area. He was a priest who went along with the expedition to minister the spiritual needs of the soldiers. Unlike so many other Spanish explorers, the commander of this mission was somewhat more enlightened, and made friends with the various Indian tribes that he encountered. Because of this, they gathered a great deal of information about this area.

"The expedition started in Mexico, and pushed up through the mountains until they arrived here. The trip to get this far, although long and arduous, was generally uneventful as far as major crises were concerned. When they arrived in the area, they encountered an Indian tribe that lived north from the valley across the ridge. This was a particularly peaceful tribe, and they spent some months with them, learning the language and becoming aquatinted with the area. From the moment they arrived, they were warned never to enter the valley. The Indians said it was inhabited by a demon that ripped its victims apart and ate their hearts."

Harry put the book on the table next to him and got up. He stood by the window, staring out into the night before continuing. "Even though the Spanish were not above superstitious tendencies themselves, they tended to regard the Indians' fears as nonsense, and generally ignored the warnings. Several months after the Spanish arrived, one of the soldiers who had been assigned to do the hunting that day didn't return. They spent several days looking for him, and finally found him in the valley. His body was shredded almost beyond recognition, and his heart had been removed." Harry returned to his chair and picked up the diary to turn another page. The brittle paper crackled like the sound of logs burning on a campfire.

"The commander still refused to believe that the attack had been done by a demon. He split his force into teams of two, and sent them to scour the entire valley for evidence of the perpetrator. These searches continued for two days until one of the teams failed to return. Since the team had been assigned to a specific area, it didn't take the commander long to find them.

"Once again the bodies had been mutilated, and the hearts removed. By the upper torso of one of the bodies, however, they found some bloody writing in the sand. One of the soldiers had managed to scrawl out a message before dying. It said 'encontre la guarida del diablo,' which translated means 'found devil's lair.' Close by they found a cave entrance that had bloody animal tracks leading into it. Since it was almost dark, and they had no material with them to make into torches, the commander decided to go back to the camp site for the night, and to return in the morning to explore the cave."

Fred was leaning forward now with his elbows on his knees as Harry continued. "When they arrived back the following morning, the commander split his group in two, leaving four men, including the priest, by the cave mouth to guard the entrance. He took six men with him to explore the inside. Evidently the cave either went back quite a ways, or there were several branches to explore, because it was almost an hour before the men at the cave opening heard anything. At first they heard only sporadic muffled musket shots, and occasionally some screams that seemed to echo from a great distance. Then there were several minutes of silence until they heard the commander's voice shouting from what appeared to be just a short distance into the cave. 'Run, run,' he screamed, 'the devil is right behind me!' This was followed by the commander's dying screams and what sounded to the priest like laughter.

"The four men at the cave mouth needed no further warnings. They turned and bolted away from the cave. The priest, who had never had any combat training or experience, was the first to lead the way. He ran faster than he imagined possible, spurred on by the occasional dying screams of the men behind him as they were snatched one by one. When the last of the three seemed to be picked away right behind him, he knew he would be next, and could sense the evil approaching him. He was too terrified to turn around and look, but just continued to run. Just as he could feel the darkness closing in on him, a sudden inspiration caused him to swing the crucifix that hung around his neck, from his chest to his back. He heard a bestial roar full of fear and hatred, and sensed the darkness falling away from him. He continued to run for several paces, then finally fell to the ground exhausted. As he fearfully raised his head to look behind him, he saw a shadow among the trees, blacker than the blackest night. Something in it studied him for awhile, then slowly melted away back into the woods.

"The priest returned to the camp and related the story to the few soldiers who had remained there on guard. That night, his sleep was haunted by nightmares and dying screams mixed with the horrible laughter he had heard when the commander had been killed. Towards morning, however, he awakened with the memory of the shadow being brought to a halt by his crucifix. He was convinced that it was an affirmation of God's omnipotence, and his duty as a priest to destroy the demon. He resolved to go back to the cave and do battle in the name of God."

Harry stopped for a while, his throat dry from all the talking. He took a sip from his drink before starting again. It had started to rain, and the sound of the heavy drops hitting the roof filled the room. A flash of lightening flooded the room with bright light, casting sharp shadows on the walls.

"When the priest communicated his plan to the remaining soldiers, they were apprehensive, but concurred that the priest was the only one with a chance against the demon. They agreed to wait one week for the priest to return, after which they would break camp and return home.

"Later that morning, armed with supplies and weapons, the priest returned to the cave. In order to travel lighter, he left the majority of his supplies underneath some bushes close by the cave. With a torch in one hand, and his crucifix held high in the other, he entered the cave. Just inside, he halted. He was consumed with fear to the point of having difficulty breathing. It took quite some time for him to regain his composure and continue onward. He explains how that moment was a turning point for him, and that the events afterwards were easier to deal with.

"The cave had several branches that wandered off in all directions, and it would have been very easy to get lost; however, the tracks on the dusty floor made it easy to find the way. He followed the twisting and meandering for some distance, at least a half-mile or so, when he turned a sharp corner and encountered a stench so fowl that he almost lost consciousness at the first breath. He stepped into a chamber that had all the decomposing bodies of his companions strewn about. The sight of the twisted and mangled bodies tossed about unnerved him, but he reminded himself of his duty and continued onward. He gingerly stepped over and around the various corpses to get to the passageway that he could see on the other side. When he reached it he was halted once again, but this time by a feeling of evil and malice so intense that he was brought down to his knees. He focused his attention on his crucifix, and slowly he was able to get back to his feet. He stepped into another chamber."

Fred jumped as a loud thunderclap burst through the night.

"He gasped as the torch light revealed the interior. Rather than the rough cave walls that he expected, he had stepped into a formal entry hall carved from rock. The hall was very large with an ornately carved pillar in the center, raising to a high ceiling. The floors and walls were polished to a deep shine, but out of a rock material the priest had never before seen. It was blood red with veins of black running through it. There were several carvings along the walls, but all were grotesque in nature, portraying nightmarish images of beast-man combinations. There were various doorways leading from the hall, but the priest dared not go any further. He felt that he entered what might be the palace of Lucifer himself, and had no desire to explore its secrets, secrets that he sensed were never meant to be seen by human eyes."

"Even though evil seemed to fill the air, he could not sense any manifestation of the demon. After his close encounter on the previous day, he was convinced that he would always be able to sense that awesome presence. He backed out of the hall and studied the entrance to it, and saw overhead a large outcropping of rock looming over it. He began to formulate a plan, and left to go back to the surface to put it into action.

"I'm going to read to you the final entry in the diary translated into English. 'I am waiting by the cave mouth for the return of the demon. When it returns, I will follow it to its lair and will attempt to destroy it, however, I fear that no earthly weapons will affect it. I will place my crucifix just inside the entrance to the hall, and will explode the keg of gunpowder I placed above the hall entryway to create a cave-in and trap the demon inside. I am resigned to the fact that I will probably die in my attempt, but feel I must cleanse the world of this foul abomination. I must get ready to go now, as I can feel the demon's approach.' "

Harry paused again, taking another drink. "After this entry is one last undated paragraph. 'As I feared, my weapons were useless. The demon was all too aware of my presence, and was waiting for me in the hall. It laughed as I fired my musket into it. When I placed my crucifix on the floor, just inside the entryway, on the little wooden stand I prepared, the demon seemed to guess my intentions. A cry of rage and fear filled the caverns. Before my eyes, the demon changed into other shapes, becoming first my commander, ordering me to remove the crucifix and throw it away. Then it became my mother as she had appeared on her deathbed, pleading with me not to leave her, terrified of eternal darkness. With a mighty effort of will, I backed away and lit the fuse to the powder keg with my torch. I miscalculated how much time I would have, for the blast came too soon, and my legs are trapped underneath rocks which I can not move. I hope that my plan was successful, and that the spawn from hell is trapped within and will remain there throughout eternity. I will leave this manuscript next to me, in the hope that if it should be found, that no one will attempt to free that which is trapped within. May God have mercy on my soul.' "

Harry closed the manuscript and fell silent for a while, immersed in his own thoughts. "You mentioned the lack of an autopsy report in the file," Harry continued. "The body had been mutilated almost beyond recognition, and the heart had been removed."

"Maybe I'll have that drink after all." Shaken, Fred went over to the bar and poured himself a tall glass of scotch. "Why wasn't any of this information kept in the file?"

"For a number of reasons, none of which should have mattered. I had just started as sheriff, and was young and ambitious. The Humphries' affair was obviously very sensational, and I saw it as a stepping stone to furthering my career. When I got a call from the governor of the state, who was a very close friend of the Humphries, I was only too willing to comply with his request to bury the investigation. Biggest mistake I ever made. All of the Governor's promises turned out to be nothing, especially when he wasn't re-elected. The guilt in leaving a murder unsolved hasn't been easy to deal with over the years."

"Harry, do you honestly believe all of this demon story?"

"I don't know what to believe. If you've got a better explanation I'm listening. There are a lot of things in this world we can't explain, Fred. What really happened at the Humphries' estate fifty years ago? I can't say for sure. I'm convinced that Humphries' wife Rachel was definitely involved up to her pretty neck, but she disappeared a few days after the murder and was never seen again. Humphries himself certainly seemed to know, but he wasn't talking. I'm also sure his son, who was about my age, also knew. After the murder, both he and his father quit traveling and never left the estate. The son is probably the only person still alive who really has any answers. If you can get him to talk after all of these years, he'd be your best bet."

Fred wasn't sure what to believe either, but it was getting late, and he needed to get some rest. He thanked Harry for being so open with him, promised to keep him posted, and left for the hotel. The rain was still coming down hard as Fred drove off.

Chapter Ten - The Claw

Fred arrived at the hotel room exhausted. He was too tired to unpack his bag. He just threw his clothes off, and fell into the bed. Even though his body was ready for sleep, his mind was still busy digesting the day's events and revelations.

Did he believe in demons? Just yesterday he would have said no. Now he wasn't so sure. He had to admit that he had no worldly explanation for all the mysteries he was dealing with. He had always been agnostic in his religious beliefs, and therefore, simply avoided the entire topic. He always felt that if the supernatural existed, someday he would discover proof. Was he now being confronted with that proof? But what proof was there really? A diary written by a superstitious priest hundreds of years ago? Who knows how the actual events had been misinterpreted so as to fit the beliefs of the time. Then there was the question of the animal prints. Even though they were unrecognizable to Janet, the fact was that they were *animal* prints. After going over all the information to date, Fred decided that a logical explanation would be found. He finally fell asleep convincing himself that the mysteries would soon be resolved.

Since Fred arrived early for breakfast the next morning, he took the liberty of selecting his favorite table in the hotel atrium coffee shop. Situated next to a large tree, the overhanging boughs provided a more intimate atmosphere than the tables out in the open. A small fountain on the other side of the tree provided the relaxing sound of running water.

Fred was enjoying a sip from his orange juice as Janet walked up. When he stood up to greet her, his breath was taken away. She was wearing a short, red sundress that accentuated her figure. Instead of being overly revealing, it allowed Fred to use his imagination. He felt his body temperature rise a few degrees. Her black hair was put up, with a few curls that dangled around her ears.

"I'm sorry I'm late," she apologized as she sat down, "but it's somewhat your fault, you know."

"How can your being late be my fault?"

"If I were meeting anyone else, I wouldn't have had to spend so much time getting ready." She lightly ran her fingertips along his arm. "After all, I made the mistake of letting you go last time. I want to make sure I don't do that again."

"Well, I'd hate for you to go to all this effort for just one breakfast. I'll bet if I try hard enough, I'm sure I could find a good excuse to come back this Saturday. Would your schedule be open for dinner then?"

"Absolutely," she answered with a coy smile. "Call me Friday afternoon and we'll set up a time."

They were interrupted by the waitress coming up to take their order. Fred was grateful. It gave him an opportunity to regain his composure.

"I've got something you might find interesting." Janet dug into her purse after the waitress left. "Later last night, I took a much closer look at the deer remains you brought in. It appears your predator left something behind when it attacked the deer. Embedded deep in one of the gashes in the deer's side, I found this."

She held up a claw. It was about two inches long and had a sharp curve to it. Its most striking characteristic, however, was its color. One often saw claws on animals that were some variation of white or black, but this claw was a glossy, blood red. It shone and glittered as Janet turned it in the light. "I've never seen anything like it. Not only is the color unusual, the shape is almost impossible. All animal claws have some imperfections in them as far as their shape and symmetry. But this thing is perfect, flawless. Also, there are no signs of wear and tear, as you would expect to find with an animal's claw. But, do you know what's really amazing?" Janet paused for effect, continuing to turn the claw in the light, keeping Fred in suspense. "Well, inside the claw I found some dried blood. Finally, I thought, something I might be able to use to figure out what left this thing behind. When I got through testing it, I couldn't believe the results. I checked and rechecked, but always came up with the same results. The blood was human blood. This claw came off a human being."

"I don't see anything unusual about that. Since it's so perfect, the claw is obviously man made. Some pervert must have attacked the deer wearing a set of claws like this. In the process of killing the animal, he probably scraped himself and left some blood in that claw."

"It's not that simple, Fred. The claw is not made of synthetic material. It definitely came from a living being. Also, if you'll look closely, you can see that it was torn away, not cut away. It got caught on one of the deer's ribs."

"That doesn't disprove what I'm saying." Fred picked up his coffee cup to take a sip. "The claw may have been torn from some animal we're not familiar with, and still used by some one who gets his jollies by slashing up animals and taking out their hearts. It's certainly a lot more plausible than some of the other scenarios I've had suggested to me."

"I hope you're right," answered Janet softly. "Because if you're wrong, you're dealing with something more deadly and calculating than anything I've ever seen." Janet took a note pad out of her bag and slashed the claw across it with little effort. Twenty pages fell to the table, cut away with neat edges.

Chapter Eleven - Joseph Humphries, III

It was late morning before Fred and Janet finished breakfast, and their reminiscing about old times. Fred decided he had learned all he could in the city, and that it was time to head back to Shady Valley. Even though he had made up his mind as to what killed the deer, he still wanted to talk to Humphries. Humphries might have some idea as to who might be responsible. This was obviously not the first time an atrocity like this had been committed.

Fred went to the nursing home first, since it was outside the town, and on his way in. The nursing facility was relatively new, and serviced several of the surrounding mountain communities.

Due to his unstable behavior, Humphries was in the secured wing of the home. He had made several attempts to leave, and the staff was concerned about his safety. He kept threatening that if they didn't let him go back to the house, they were all as good as dead.

"Fred, it's always nice to see you." The on-duty nurse looked up with a smile as Fred walked in. "Are you going to be staying with us for a while?"

"Lucy, I'd be more than you could handle."

"If I were ten years younger, I'd take you up on that. Have you ever considered the benefits of an older woman." Lucy gave him a sly a wink.

"If I do, you're first on my list." He leaned down with his elbows on the counter, and tried to look as serious as possible.

"Tease! What brings you here today?"

"I thought I'd stop by and talk to Mr. Humphries. You called me a few days ago asking me to do so, remember?"

"That's right, we're a little concerned." Lucy leaned back, her chair making a loud squeak. "Not only does he keep warning us we're all in danger, but he keeps going on about his mother, and how he let her down. When we try to get more details out of him, he just clams up. Since his mother was involved in that murder investigation, way back when, I thought you might want to try and see if he'll open up to you better than he does to us."

Fred was shocked when he walked into Humphries' room and got a look at him. He had heard that the man had not aged well, but couldn't believe how old and decrepit he appeared. Granted, Joseph Humphries, III was seventy-five, but he looked to be in his nineties. He was pale, gaunt, and extremely wrinkled. The light blue pajamas hung from his shriveled frame. His posture was stooped, and his body had the shakes. He huddled on the single bed that stood in the center of the room. A small nightstand, dresser, and chair were the only other pieces of furniture in the room. A shaded lamp on the dresser filled the room with a soft glow that illuminated the white walls and floor.

"Mr. Humphries." Fred spoke in a loud voice, trying to get his attention. "I came by to talk to you. I hope maybe you can shed some light on a situation I'm trying to resolve."

Humphries looked up and studied Fred intently, but there was no indication as to what he was thinking behind his smoldering eyes. He coughed loudly.

"We found a deer that had been killed up above town. It appears that it was killed the same way your servant was fifty years ago."

Humphries dark brown eyes grew as he heard the news. A shiver went through his body, but he still made no indication that he was going to break his silence.

Exasperated, Fred grabbed Humphries' shoulders and crouched down to look into his eyes. "You've got to tell me what happened fifty years ago. What if the next victim is a child? Do you want that on your conscience? You're the only one left who knows what happened. You're the only one left who can help."

Humphries looked down, avoiding Fred's eyes, and continued his silence. Fred stood up and turned around to leave, resigned he wasn't getting anywhere. Just as he approached the door, Humphries began speaking very softly.

"If you had left me in my home, you wouldn't be having this problem. But now that she's broken out, even I can't help you." He fell quiet again, and began to sob softly. Fred turned and sat down in the chair, waiting patiently for Humphries to regain his composure.

"Sheriff, if we had told you the truth fifty years ago, you wouldn't have believed us. I doubt if you'll believe me now either."

"Why don't you try me. After all the stories I've heard in the past couple of days, I doubt anything would surprise me.

Harry, the sheriff who handled the investigation, had an old Spanish diary that talked about a demon in the valley. So, believe me, I'm ready to listen to anything."

"So that's where the diary went. My father and I always wondered what had happened to it. We searched the entire house for it. I'm sure your reaction to that diary was the same as mine when I first read it sixty years ago. You can't imagine how much I wish I had never seen that infernal book. Unfortunately, my family discovered it, and the story told in it turned out to be true, completely true."

Humphries collapsed in a fit of coughing, and it took some time before he could continue. "My grandfather built the house in the mid nineteenth century. He traveled quite a bit, and was always impressed with the old European castles he came across. So as much as his budget would allow, he tried to bring part of Europe to the valley, here in the mountains. And just like many of the European castles, the house is honeycombed with secret stairways and passageways. In the process of digging an underground passageway to the guesthouse, they broke through into a cave. They followed it to a chamber that was filled with skeletons. At the far end, there appeared to have been a cave-in that partially covered one of the skeletons. They found the diary under one of its arms.

"Since most of the workmen could not even read English, much less Spanish, they took the diary to my grandfather. Being fluent in several languages, he easily translated it. He wasn't sure he totally believed the story, but he saw no reason to disturb all the skeletal remains. He told the workmen that it was a cave-in site of old miners, and had them brick off the cave entrance from the passageway. If he had only destroyed the diary itself, everything might still have turned out all right. But he didn't. He kept it in the library as a curiosity.

Also, he figured that some day it might have considerable historical value. The bloody fool!"

Humphries fell silent and rocked back and forth on the bed, his head shaking side to side as he started once again. "Years later, my father married my mother to be, and moved her into the house. My grandfather had already passed away, so my mother was left to her own devices during my father's long business trips. He would be gone months at a time, checking on the various foreign investments he had made. He never would trust anyone else.

"It was during this time that she discovered the diary in the library. Being curious by nature, she found the diary fascinating, and explored the underground passageway to see if she could find the bricked off entrance. She found it easily enough, since the workmen had not made any special efforts to hide it. She decided to have it opened, but then found out she was pregnant with me. All thoughts of the diary were put aside as she prepared for the new arrival. She was the best mother any child could hope for. She was loving, attentive, and raised me the best she could. We became very close.

"When I went off to college, her loneliness set in once again. My father still traveled extensively and just wasn't around much. It wasn't long before she remembered the diary, and this time there was nothing to distract her. She took one of the servants into her confidence, and had him open up the cave. Just as the diary described, it led to the cavern with all the skeletal remains, and the cave-in at the end.

"Rather than immediately opening up the cave-in, she decided to do some research on witchcraft and demonology. If there actually was a demon there, she didn't want to face it unprepared. Since I was at the university, she wrote to me, and asked me to send her as many books as possible on those topics.

She wrote that she wished to help one of the servants who was unusually superstitious, and convinced that a demon was trying to possess him. Since I was used to my mother being concerned for others, I thought nothing of it, and arranged for boxes of books to be sent to her. She obviously pursued other resources as well, because within a couple of years she managed to amass an enormous library on the occult. That library is still there in one of the secret underground rooms under the house."

Humphries paused to take a sip of water from the glass next to him on the nightstand. His hand shook so badly that he left a small trail of water droplets on the sheets of the bed. "She obviously did a considerable amount of research in that time, and discovered knowledge that she felt would protect her from the demon. I never did find out what it was. She had the servant clear out the cave-in. When all the rocks were cleared away, she sent the servant back up to the house. She took the lantern, and proceeded through the opened passageway. She only went in a short distance when she encountered the crucifix left by the Spanish priest. It was still there, keeping the terror within from emerging. She sat down there, by the crucifix, knowing that she would always be safe within its proximity. She did not call out. She knew that the demon would be aware of her presence, and would sooner or later come to investigate. She did not have long to wait. The demon did indeed appear, but kept its distance from the crucifix."

Once again he buried his head in his hands and cried out. "Mother, Mother, whatever were you thinking?" He sobbed for a while, and Fred waited patiently for him to calm back down and continue.

"They talked for some time together," he said through his tears. "She, trying to learn as much from it as she could, and the demon hoping that it could convince her to remove the crucifix. This ultimately led to her downfall. She thought that the knowledge she could learn from the demon, knowledge that spanned countless centuries, could be used to do good. How could she have been so foolish? The demon proved to be very personable. Over time, it began to weave its own insidious will into her thoughts. My mother had always been somewhat vain, and indeed, she was a very beautiful woman. The demon tempted her with eternal beauty and eternal life. She began to listen to its promises, and her mind was slowly twisted into a receptacle for the demon's wishes. My mother did indeed learn a great deal, but the lessons were not meant for mortal beings. She couldn't assimilate all the new information and retain her sanity. She did, however, retain one rational thought. She refused to remove the crucifix from the opening, realizing that the demon would destroy her."

Humphries had quit crying, and was now unusually steady. "The demon was willing to bide its time, knowing it would some day take control of her completely. Following the demon's instructions, she cleared the skeletal remains in the cavern to one side, and constructed an altar for satanic rituals. At first, only animals were sacrificed on the altar, but one day, she finally succumbed to the demon's pressure, and brought her trusted servant down to be a human sacrifice. He tried to resist, but by this time my mother had learned how to alter her shape, and she became a strong beast-like creature, not unlike the demon.

"The poor man was brutally tormented and killed. His heart was removed, and my mother tossed it to the demon, who considered it a delicacy. My mother must have felt some guilt for what she had done since she couldn't bear to see the dead man's body in the cavern, rotting away. She took the body and hid it in the woods, but it was soon discovered and the investigation began. My father and I returned home when we got the news. Since I had recently graduated, I had been traveling with him so I could learn more about the family investments.

"We were horrified at what we discovered when we got home. My father pulled some strings at the governor's office to bury the official investigation, but our own investigation continued until we uncovered the truth. Being familiar with all of the house's secret passageways, it didn't take us long to discover my mother's secret library. By going through her notes, we were able to piece together what had happened. Where she herself had fled to we couldn't discover. We followed the cave as far as the chamber but could not find her. We were certain she would eventually reestablish contact with the demon, so we proceeded to set a trap for her."

Fred shivered. The air in the room seemed to turn colder as the story unfolded.

"We built a cage just inside the passageway to the cavern, and baited it with one of her most prized possessions. Inside, on a table, we placed a locket that had once belonged to her mother. Next to it we put a lantern, to attract her attention.

"In her notes, she had theorized that holy water might have the same effect on the demon that the crucifix did. We decided to test her theory, but on her instead. We ran a very shallow trough along the bottom of the cage bars. We obtained, from a Catholic Church, a large jar of holy water. We had to lie a little to get so much. We used the excuse that the closest Catholic Church, at that time, was over forty miles from our house.

"We took turns setting up a watch for her just inside the darkness of the cave itself. After a couple of days, she showed up on my watch. She was in her own form, but seemed to be in a trance. She walked past the doorway to the cage, and I was afraid she would walk right into me, when she turned her head and looked towards the table with the lantern. She walked over to it, and picked up the locket. For a moment, the hardened expression on her face seemed to soften as a tear ran down her cheek.

"Not daring to wait any longer, I sprang up, ran over and slammed the cage door shut. I could hardly believe my eyes when I saw her change shape to demon form. Her arms became longer and more muscular. Large sharp claws grew from her fingertips. Her face was transformed into a hideous shape, with fangs jutting over her lower lip. She threw herself into the cage bars, and they began to bend apart as she started pulling on them. Almost too late, I grabbed the jar of holy water that was close by, and poured it through the bars into the trough. Instantly, she jumped back, shouting out a growl of anger. My father heard the commotion and ran down. He stood frozen in amazement at the sight of his once beloved wife. Something in him seemed to snap at that point, and he was never the same man afterwards. He always blamed himself for the entire affair, insisting that if he had only traveled less, or taken his wife with him on the trips, that the whole mess would never have taken place.

"After talking about the situation for a few days, my father and I decided that it would be our task to take care of Mother for the rest of her life. We realized the amount of holy water it took to keep the trough filled was too much to acquire on a regular basis, without arousing suspicion from the church. After some experimentation, we found we could mix a very small amount into her drinking water, and that it kept the evil within her sufficiently weakened from attempting to escape. Unlike the demon, my mother was still mortal, and needed to eat and drink in order to exist. So as to make our job easier, my father donated the land and supplied the funds for the Catholic Church to be built across the street from the house. I made it a habit to go to mass every morning, and fill a small bottle of it for use on my mother.

"My father turned his thoughts inward, more and more. Eventually, after a few years, he fell into a deep depression and tired to commit suicide. He was not totally successful, and it took several days before he died. On his deathbed, I promised I would continue to guard Mother until her death."

At this point Humphries once again began to sob. He had begun to sweat towards the end of his story, and his lank gray hair stuck to his head. His pajamas were molded around his bony arms and legs. "I failed. May God forgive me, I failed. And now more people are going to die."

"Who else is going to die?"

"Mother told me the demon had been waiting centuries for someone to appear that would have the power to destroy it, and that the person had finally come. She told me that if I would only let her out, she could make this person's powers her own, and destroy the demon herself. Then, she thought, she would become immortal in its place. Her mind just wasn't the same anymore."

"Who was this person?" Fred was insistent, becoming concerned.

"She was convinced it was Jake and Ellen's boy, Randy."

"Randy! Randy's just a kid. You've got to be kidding."

But Humphries had fallen silent. After considerable coaxing, he gave Fred a brief description of the secret passageways in the house, then would not say any more. Fred quietly got up, put his hand on Humphries shoulder, thanked him for his help, and left. He felt the old man needed some time to make peace with his memories. More importantly, however, Fred needed get over to Jake and Ellen's. If even a small portion of this story were remotely true, they were all in grave danger.

Chapter Twelve - The Chamber

Fred raced from the nursing home. Throughout Humphries' story, a sense of dread started to overcome him. He couldn't shake the feeling that something terrible had happened to Randy. Also, the revelation that the main house and guest house were connected by an underground passageway only served to underline the entire family's danger.

Fred's own thoughts were in total turmoil. He no longer knew what to believe. All of the pieces of the puzzle fit together, but what an unbelievable picture they formed. In spite of his agnosticism, he found himself praying to God to keep Randy and his family safe. His whole world seemed to be falling apart, and he no longer knew where to turn.

Even though it seemed like an eternity, the drive to Randy's only took thirty minutes. He pulled into the driveway and ran to the front door. Since it was close to dinnertime, he hoped that Ellen at least would be home. He was about to ring the doorbell when Jake pulled in the driveway next to Fred's Jeep.

"Fred," called Jake, as he got out of his car. "Back from the city already? What did you find out about the critter that's supposedly stalking the town?"

"Jake, if I told you, you wouldn't believe me. Do you know where Ellen and Randy are?"

"I assume Ellen's inside cooking dinner, or at least I hope so. I have to admit, for some reason I'm starving tonight. Why don't you join us, and you can tell us over supper what you learned in the city. I haven't seen Randy all day. Ellen must know where he is." Jake opened the front door and held it for Fred. Stepping in the hallway, they were surprised to hear Thunder howling.

Ellen came out of the kitchen, and walked down the hall to greet them. "I'm glad you're here." Her hair was out of place and she was perspiring. "When I got home, I found Thunder howling in the basement, but for some reason, he won't come out when I open the door. Maybe you can figure out what's wrong with that dog."

"Ellen, do you know where Randy is?" asked Fred.

"No. I looked around for him, but couldn't find him. I was hoping he'd be with one of you two."

Just then Rachel came out of the living room, and started down the hallway towards her room.

"*Rachel!*" Fred stared at the little girl. "*You* can't be here, that's not possible. I ran into you and your parents in the city last night."

"I don't know how you could have." Ellen was busy wiping her brow with her apron. "Rachel's been here with us for the past few days."

"Rachel," whispered Fred softly to himself, as if trying to figure something out. Fred took a step towards her, and before everyone's eyes, she changed into a beast-like creature.

Her clothes ripped from her body as she began to tower over them. Coarse fur covered her body, reeking with a foul stench. Fangs jutted over her lips, and a large snout covered her face. Long, muscular arms bulging with corded muscles hung almost to the floor. Long blood-red claws spouted from her paws and feet. With a bestial cry of rage she swung one of her paws towards Ellen. Hit in the shoulder, Ellen crashed into the wall with a sickening crunch. She fell like a broken doll. Before Jake or Fred could react, the creature fled down the hall, and out the back door. Fred drew his gun, and was prepared to chase after it, when Jake, who was tending to Ellen, stopped him.

"Fred, we've got to get Ellen to the hospital. Her head hit the wall, and her scalp is bleeding real bad."

Fred put his gun back in the holster, and knelt down to take a look at Ellen. He didn't like what he saw. She was unconscious and the whole side of her head was a mass of blood, with small patches of white skull showing through the torn scalp. He couldn't tell if the skull was fractured, but at the very least she had suffered a massive concussion with the possibility of internal bleeding.

"Jake, pick her up as gently as you can, and let's get her out to the Jeep."

Jake did as instructed, and together they got her out to his vehicle. Jake held her in his lap, a stunned look on his face. Fred backed out of the driveway and raced towards the hospital, only a short distance away.

"Jake, when we're at the hospital, let me do the talking. If we told them the truth about what happened, they wouldn't believe it."

"I'm not sure I believe what happened." Jake cradled his wife, tears flowing down his cheeks.

"It's a long story, Jake. Since the hospital is just around the corner, I don't have time to tell you. Bear with me until we get Ellen situated. Then I'll give you the details as quick as I can."

At the hospital, Fred burst though the emergency room doors. He told the doctor that Ellen had been injured by a prowler in the house, and that they needed to get back as soon as possible since Randy was still missing. As they stood impatiently in the waiting room, Fred told Jake all that he had discovered so far. Jake listened, his face drawn. He made no comment as Fred laid out the entire story, beginning with the missionary priest's diary, and bringing it to the present with Humphries' tale.

"If I hadn't seen Rachel turn into that creature with my own eyes, I wouldn't believe a word you told me. But if Rachel does have Randy, how do we know he's still alive?"

"We don't know, for sure." Fred put his hand on Jake's shoulder. "But somehow I have a feeling he is. Both Rachel and the demon were waiting for Randy to come to Shady Valley. The demon's been waiting for centuries. When Rachel broke loose, she decided to precipitate matters and go after him herself. The way Humphries explained it I just can't imagine her purpose was to kill him outright. If she had wanted to do that, why bother with the elaborate masquerade? She had several opportunities very early on."

They were interrupted by the doctor. "It looks as though Ellen will be all right. She took a rather nasty blow to the head. We did a CAT scan, and there's no internal bleeding as far as I can tell. She's conscious, but still very groggy and disoriented. She'll feel much better in the morning. You can go in and see her if you like, but please don't spend more than a few minutes with her. She needs all the rest she can get right now. After you've seen her, you might as well go look for your son. There's not much else you can do here."

They found Ellen on the emergency room bed, all bandaged up. As the doctor had warned, she was very groggy. Her eyes fluttered open briefly, and she smiled as Jake gave her hand a squeeze, then drifted away. Jake kissed her lightly on the cheek, and softly whispered, "I love you."

They went to Fred's office first in order to arm themselves. When they arrived, Fred went right to the gun cabinet and selected two shot guns, handing one to Jake.

"Hopefully, these will give Rachel some second thoughts." Fred grabbed several boxes of shells. "Humphries mentioned that even though the demon is immortal, Rachel is not. Grab those flashlights." He stuffed some extra shells into his pockets. " Where do you think we should start?"

"Let's start at the house. Randy would never lock Thunder in the basement. There's got to be some reason why the dog's down there."

They raced back to the house. It was starting to get dark, and the full moon was rising. A light breeze was blowing away the day's residual heat. The stars were etched against the clear sky.

"Fred, I don't know what I would do if something happened to Randy. I'm not sure I could handle it. That boy is everything to me. He's part of me."

"Hang in there." Fred gave Jake's shoulder a squeeze. "I've always considered Randy to be the son I never had. I'll do everything I can."

They arrived at the house and entered the front door cautiously. Having witnessed Rachel's strength and speed, they were not about to rush in anywhere. After turning on lights and checking the main floor thoroughly, they opened the door to the basement to let Thunder out. The dog was happy to see them, but appeared agitated, and wouldn't leave the stairway.

Jake hugged Thunder. "Thunder, do you know where Randy is? We need to find Randy."

Thunder immediately turned and headed back down the stairs. Jake and Fred followed as Thunder led them down the basement hallway to the large room at the end. He walked up to the wall at the end and started pawing it.

Jake started to study the wall. "Last night Randy and I ended up down here because we both thought we had heard noises in the basement. The only thing we could find was this rat hole. I wonder if maybe what we heard was Rachel going into the passageway back to the main house. There's got to be a way through this wall."

Try as they might, however, they could not get the wall open. Even though they found the loose rock along the top of the wall, and the handle inside it, the wall appeared to be stuck. The handle was pulled, so the locking mechanism must have been released, but the wall would only move back a few inches until it stopped.

Fred wiped the perspiration from his forehead. "I wonder if there's something jamming it on the other side. Let's head over to the main house and see if we can get in from that side."

They proceeded to leave, but were surprised that Thunder would not come with them. The animal was determined to stay there and wait for Randy's return. He knew Randy was in there, and he wasn't going to abandon him.

Leaving the stubborn St. Bernard behind, they made their way over the grounds to the main house. Even though it was now completely dark, the moonlight was strong enough for them to see clearly.

The shadows cast by the large trees gave everything a ghostlike appearance. The main house also, looked macabre in the moonlight. The turrets shone against the night sky.

They quietly went up the steps to the front doors. The only noise they could hear was the soft sound of crickets, chirping in the night. Fred shone the flashlight on the lock box as Jake leaned down to open it. His hands trembled slightly as he turned the dial. After entering the combination, the box opened with a snap. Jake took out the key and opened the door. It opened noiselessly into the front hall. The moonlight coming in through the windows illuminated patches of the floor and walls, but did nothing to lift the eerie darkness from inside the house. Using flashlights, they entered with Fred leading the way. The floorboards creaked as they softly made their way into the house. The echoes faded silently into the darkness.

"Humphries told me the easiest way to get into the underground passageway was through the library fireplace," whispered Fred softly.

They crept quietly though the hall and across the library to the fireplace. Here Fred searched for the lever high up on the right inside wall where Humphries had told him he would find it. Discovering it, he gave a hard pull, and the locking mechanism released with a sharp click. The wall swung open noiselessly.

They peered down the steep stairs with their flashlights, then entered the narrow stairway single file. They continued to the bottom in silence and turned the corner into the subterranean chamber.

"This is Rachel's secret library. Fred shone his flashlight around the room. "I wish we could take the time to look for her notes. I'm sure they'd answer a lot of questions."

"Where do we go from here?"

"The wooden door over there is supposed to open into the passageway that connects the two houses. It also opens into the cave that leads to the demon, where Rachel constructed her altar. Even though that's the last place I'd care to explore, I'll bet that's going to be our best bet."

Opening the door proved to be difficult. It had been torn from the two lower hinges, but still hung from the top hinge. It had to be partially lifted before they could swing it open. Constructed out of solid hardwood, two inches thick, it weighed a considerable amount, and took both of them to move it.

As they illuminated the cavern within, both of them were amazed to see the steel bars that spanned half the interior. Even though they had both heard the story of Rachel, it was still difficult to accept. Seeing physical proof was like entering a nightmare while still being wide-awake.

Jake shone his flashlight around the interior. "That must be where Humphries kept his mother all those years. For the life of me, I can't imagine what Humphries and his father were thinking. No matter what she became, even death would have been kinder than locking her up in this cage all those years."

"Sometimes people don't realize they're thinking of themselves when they do things like this. They're not ready to let go of a loved one, so in the name of mercy, they torture the one they're trying to protect."

They carefully filed past the bars into the passageway on the other side. Even though there didn't appear to be any immediate danger, neither one of them could shake the feeling of malice that seemed to permeate the air around them. It was as if their presence was offensive to the environment.

They stubbornly persisted onward, casting nervous glances around them. They soon came to the branch. On the right, the finished passageway continued onward to the guesthouse. On the left, the unfinished cave beckoned to them with the hope of finding Randy. Resolutely, they entered the cave and forged into the darkness.

Their flashlights didn't seem to shine as brightly here as in the passageway. The darkness was so heavy that it seemed as though they could reach out and touch it. As they continued onward, the feeling of dread and oppression grew with every step. It wasn't long before they labored just to keep going. The air soon became foul with the smell of rotted flesh and the stench made breathing difficult. They had almost lost hope of ever seeing an end to their journey in the darkness, when they could make out a faint light ahead. They continued as quietly as possible, not wishing to alert whatever was there.

Soon the light flickered along the walls. They turned off the flashlights, and took hold of the shotguns more tightly. Abruptly, they came to a turn and saw a large chamber before them.

Their worst imaginings could not have prepared them for the sight that lay before them. Several large torches were set in the walls all the way around the chamber. Human skeletons were hung on the walls. The chamber itself was oval in shape, forty feet by thirty feet. In the center was a large stone altar that appeared to have been carved out of a solid piece of black rock. They were horrified to see the bound and gagged form of Randy lying on the slab. All sorts of arcane symbols decorated the floor surrounding the altar. At one side of the altar stood Rachel, not in her beast-like demon form, but as herself.

She had obviously been able to cheat time so far. She appeared to be in her mid forties, and very attractive. Long blond hair cascaded over her slender shoulders. She seemed physically trim, almost athletic in her build. A graceful, but hardened face was bent towards Randy in concentration. Fred and Jake were about to step into the chamber when a voice that seemed to emanate from the depths of the earth boomed forth.

"Rachel, why are you persisting in this insanity? Is it not enough that I have granted you power and long life far beyond your dreams? Kill the boy and be done with it. What do you hope to accomplish?"

"Do not toy with me, Gorshault." Rachel was flipping through the pages of a large book that was placed next to Randy. "Only too well do I know your purpose. From the very first, it has been your sole intent to have me remove the crucifix and free you from your prison. Do you take me for a complete fool? As soon as you're free, your first act would be to slay me."

"You misjudge me, Rachel. With you at my side, we can go forth and carve out an empire. Others will worship and serve us. Free me and we will begin our conquest together. We will kill this boy and be done with him. He means nothing."

"He means nothing?" Rachel laughed. "For years you have been foretelling his arrival, warning me that someone would come who would one day destroy you. You implored me to break out of my own prison, so that I could kill this person as a boy, before his power became apparent. Now you would have me believe that he means nothing? I am not so foolish."

"Rachel, hear me!" The voice thundered and shook the floor beneath their feet. "The boy means nothing because he has not yet developed his power. Even I do not know when that will happen or what form it will take. But at this point, either one of us can easily kill him. Free me, my love, and we can spend eternity together."

"Your love? The only one you love, Gorshault, is yourself. You do not love me. You only see me as a means to an end. This boy will fulfill my desire for more power. Even though his power has not yet manifested itself, he must already have it. I can sense that he is different from others. And, if his power is sufficient to destroy the mighty immortal Gorshault himself, then nothing will be able to stand in my way, including you. Now be still, I have work to do."

"Rachel, Rachel, is this how you repay me? I am concerned only for your safety. You do not yet possess the skill to do what you are attempting. The assimilation of another's thoughts, memories, the essence of their being, is a very difficult undertaking, fraught with perils for one who lacks both the skill and power. Do not try this."

Having heard enough, Fred motioned for Jake to go around to the right, while he proceeded to the left. He hoped one of them might catch Rachel off guard. They were not that fortunate. Rachel immediately spun around towards them and changed into her beast form. She laid the claws from one paw across Randy's throat.

"Well if it isn't father to the rescue, aided by his loyal friend, the sheriff," sneered Rachel, her fangs dripping saliva on Randy's arm. "Unless you'd like me to tear open Randy's throat, stop where you are and lay your weapons gently on the ground."

The sound of Rachel's feminine voice coming from the hideous beast was unnerving. Shaken, Fred and Jake carefully laid their shotguns down on the ground beside them.

Jake dropped to his knees. "Please. Don't harm my son. Randy has no special powers. He's only a boy."

"Quiet, and do as I say. Sheriff, take your handcuffs from your belt, and handcuff Jake's right hand to his left ankle. Then come slowly towards me."

Fred did as instructed hoping Rachel wouldn't notice him taking a handful of dirt in his right hand while he was handcuffing Jake's hand to his ankle. He kept coming towards Rachel until he was about six feet away. Then quick as he could, he threw the dirt in Rachel's eyes. She let out a howl, and brought her arms up to protect her face. In the process of snatching her claws from Randy, she ripped the gag from Randy's face, leaving an ugly gash in his cheek. Randy let out a scream at the top of his lungs. Fred lunged towards Randy, hoping to scoop him off the altar. Rachel recovered more quickly than he hoped. She caught Fred with one of her arms and sent him flying across the chamber where he crumpled against one of the walls. He started to get up when Rachel sent a burst of energy from one of her arms that exploded inside him. He found he was paralyzed and couldn't move.

Rachel turned her attention back to Randy, who was sobbing from fear. She tore his shirt open and laid her claws on his chest. "When I rip your chest open, I will plunge my arms deep into your body. When I pull them out, I will draw your life force out with them and absorb it into my own."

She raised her claws above Randy's chest, and Randy screamed in terror. She was about to tear into his body, when 240 pounds of sheer fury crashed into her.

Thunder had heard Randy's cry of pain when the gag had been torn from his face. How the dog could possibly have heard anything through all the solid rock that separated them, will always remain a mystery. Leaping into action, the animal crashed against the wall, throwing his immense frame into the barrier. The board that had been jammed into it on the other side snapped like a twig, and the wall had crashed inward. Following his instinct, Thunder had run at breakneck speed to help his friend.

With her attention focused on Randy, Rachel had not seen the dog come charging across the chamber. The dog ran into her with the force of a train, knocking her completely off her feet. The two rolled head over heels across the chamber floor. Rachel tried to bring her razor sharp claws to her defense, but she was too late. Thunder closed his jaws over Rachel's throat, and with a surge of his powerful muscles, snapped her neck like a twig. Rachel gave an astonished cry, and went limp.

Fred found his paralysis gone the instant Rachel died. He painfully got to his feet and went over to check on Randy. Randy was crying uncontrollably, and threw his arms around Fred as soon as he was untied. Thunder came up and rubbed his head against Randy's side, happy to see that he was all right. Fred then went to Jake, unlocked the handcuffs that kept him immobilized, and helped him to his feet. Jake raced over to Randy, tears streaming down his face. He threw his arms around his son, crying out in happiness.

Fred cautiously checked Rachel, but found only the remains of an old woman, shriveled beyond recognition. The spell that maintained her youth had broken at the instant of her death.

Their joy was brought to an abrupt halt, when a cold laugh filled the chamber.

"Enjoy your victory while you can. Rachel was only a shadow of what you will someday have to face. You and I are destined to meet again Randy. I, for one, am looking forward to that encounter."

They all looked over to the source of the voice. Ten feet away was the doorway to the demon's lair. All evidence of the rockslide that had covered the entryway had been removed. An ornately carved arch, ten feet tall, led a short distance to the under-ground palace. In the center of the archway, the missionary priest's crucifix still stood, securely in place on a little wooden stand. A few feet beyond the crucifix stood the demon itself. It was difficult to say what its shape was. A shadow cloaked it in a veil of secrecy. It radiated a sense of ultimate power, corrupted by the evil it had taken upon itself. Even Thunder growled softly and backed away from the towering shadow.

Fred moved them all away from the demon and back into the cave. As he got to the shotguns, he aimed one at the roof of the chamber, and let loose with a barrage of blasts. A rumble started to fill the air, and with a deafening crash the entire roof of the chamber collapsed. Fearing a general cave-in, they ran back up the cave to the passageway as rocks fell around their heads.

Chapter Thirteen - Buried

Randy breathed a sigh of relief as the last brick was set into place. For the past several weeks, he had helped his father and Fred seal away all evidence of the horrors that they had encountered underground. Rebuilding the wall in their basement had been relatively simple compared to the task of sealing all the entryways in the main house. The library fireplace was rebuilt, and the entry panels in each of the bedroom dressing rooms were sealed, with the coat-hook trigger mechanisms disconnected.

They all agreed to keep the entire affair a secret. Not only were they convinced that no one would believe them, they did not want to take the risk of someone digging out the underground chamber and releasing the horror that was buried there. Luckily, very few people knew that something out of the ordinary had happened. Ellen was released from the hospital a couple of days later, and after hearing Jake's explanation, was only too happy to forget the events of the past few days. Even though Jake offered to show her the underground passageways, she had no desire to see them.

Janet was another matter, however. After Fred failed to call her on Friday, as he had promised, she showed up on her own. Being told that Fred was busy helping Jake do some work on the Humphries house, she found them there, busy rebuilding the fireplace. She wasn't about to believe the explanation Fred had told the townsfolk, that he had trapped and killed the mountain lion that had killed the deer. Realizing that nothing less than the complete truth would satisfy her, Fred showed her all the underground passageways, and told her the entire story of what had happened. Even though she was fascinated, she agreed that the truth should be kept secret.

Humphries was happy to learn that his mother had finally passed away, and that he would be able to live the rest of his life in relative peace. Fred convinced the courts that Humphries was sane, and that a guardian was not needed. Accordingly, the profits realized from the sale of the main house, when it finally sold, would be enough for him to retire on.

Jake and Ellen also decided to put their house up for sale. Randy had not fared so well. He still had nightmares, and even seemed to hear the demon's voice in his head while awake. They hoped that a change of scenery away from the valley might help him put the entire matter behind him.

Deep underground, Gorshault was once again trapped. He didn't care. He could bide his time, knowing that he would soon be free again. What were a few years to a being that had existed since the beginning of the world?

PART TWO - GORSHAULT

Chapter One - Discovery

Chris had been digging in this side tunnel for five days now. He and his fellow archeologist, Roger, began exploring this network of caves in Shady Valley a few months ago. They were studying how the Indian tribes of the region lived several hundred years ago, and became interested in the caves when local residents had spoken of having found bones and skeletal remains in them. It had taken a great deal of initial exploration just to map the network in order to determine where the best areas to search were located. The network was a mixture of natural caves and mining tunnels that had been added later during the gold rush. That very fact was the cause of disagreement between Chris and Roger.

They stumbled upon a blocked off tunnel that branched off one of the smaller mining tunnels. Since they were not interested in checking out the man-made tunnels that were dug long after the Indians had left the area, they would have disregarded the blocked off tunnel had it not been for Chris. He noticed some lettering etched into the wall that read, "Warning - Haunted."

Roger dismissed it as being nothing more than the scrawls of some overly superstitious miner who had imagined some strange noises, but Chris was not convinced. His gut feeling told him there was more to it than that, and he intended to find out. As Roger had vehemently protested wasting his time on what he felt was groundless nonsense, Chris found himself digging out the opening on his own. Roger pursued other explorations he thought showed more potential.

The blocked-off tunnel was carefully sealed, with the blockage going back several feet. Consequently, it took days of backbreaking lifting and hauling before the blockage was removed, and Chris was able to enter it freely.

He went in nervously, continually checking out the roof with his flashlight. Even though it appeared to cut through solid rock, the possibility of being buried alive in the heart of the mountain was not a concept that Chris particularly relished. After moving along cautiously for twenty feet, he was surprised to find that the tunnel ended except for a small opening at the ground only three feet tall. Getting on his hands and knees, he crawled through the opening and emerged into a larger, natural cave. Getting up, he looked around the larger cave, studying exactly where the opening was. He was glad he had done so. The tunnel opening was underneath a shelf-like protrusion of rock, and would have been nearly impossible to find without suitable marking. Taking a can of spray paint out of his pack, he made a large bright yellow arrow, marking the side of the wall. Roger would not have approved the defacing of the cave wall, but Chris did not care. He was concerned with his own safety, and could not see how the wall of the cave could possibly present any archeological value. Besides, a little turpentine would clean most of it up.

Chris trembled with the excitement that was building up inside him. He was certain he was onto something big. He looked forward to boasting of his success to Roger, who always thought he "knew better," and most often was justified by more than his share of good fortune. In the two years they had worked together, Chris always seemed to be in Roger's shadow, and was beginning to heartily resent it. What Chris sometimes forgot, was that at the age of thirty-two, he lacked the experience of Roger, nearly fifteen years older.

He proceeded to his left first, and went 200 feet before he found that the cave opened into a man-made passageway that was constructed of precisely laid stones. Even though the origin of the passageway intrigued him, he was more interested in finding ancient artifacts, and felt the chances of finding them in a natural cave were much greater. He could always explore the passageway later at his convenience. There again, Roger would have proceeded more slowly, carefully examining everything as he came to it. But Chris was impatient to make a big find, and didn't want to waste his time on petty discoveries.

He doubled back and followed the cave deeper into the mountain. It was fairly large, and he had no trouble making good progress. He had gone a fair distance, approximately 1,000 feet, when he ran into another obstacle. Obviously, a cave-in had occurred and his path was blocked by a pile of fallen rocks. Disheartened, he was about to turn back when he noticed what appeared to be a sliver of an opening at the roof of the cave. Excited, he carefully pulled out some of the rocks along the roof, and shining his light into the opening saw what appeared to be a large cavern on the other side. As far as he could make out, it seemed that except for some large rocks that were scattered about on the cavern floor, his only obstacle was the pile of rocks in front of him, which didn't seem to be more than six feet across. What had really gotten the adrenaline flowing, however, were the glimpses he had gotten of markings on the cavern floor, and skeletons along the walls.

He threw himself at the pile of rocks with enthusiasm that was fueled by visions of success and glory. He could just imagine the accolades that would be piled on his shoulders by his colleagues, and how envious Roger would be. Finally he would receive the rewards due him for his diligence and foresight.

Since many of the stones in the pile were quite large, it took the better part of an hour to clear out an opening large enough to crawl through. One rock in particular was almost three feet across, and it took every ounce of strength he had to roll it out of the way.

When he finally made it through and turned up the lamp, the sight that met his eyes took his breath away. The stone altar in the middle, surrounded by the strange markings on the floor, was unlike anything he had ever seen. Skeletons hung on the walls like hunting trophies in a predator's gallery. Chris could understand that superstitious miners, having stumbled into the cavern, would have fled and considered the whole area as being haunted. The stench alone would have been enough to deter them. Even though the skeletons were devoid of any flesh, the rancid odor of decaying bodies hung in the air.

For himself, Chris did not believe in such nonsense. He felt that religious and superstitious idiocy was best left to the religious fanatics that obviously lacked the common sense that science offered. Every mystery, he liked to argue, had a rational scientific explanation. One only had to look hard enough to find it. And if the explanation could not be found, it was simply because all of the information on the mystery had not yet been ascertained. He maintained that the only reason such a large percentage of the populace persisted in their belief of a supreme deity was because of groundless fears based on their lack of understanding of the world around them. When ignorance and fear are finally resolved, he always concluded, religion will loose its purpose and die away.

His initial reaction to the cavern was that he had stumbled onto a site used for pagan rituals and possible human sacrifice. The notion excited him. He looked at the altar, and wondered how many fools had lost their lives there, dying in vain for naught. The Indians of this region were believed to be peaceful, and not known to practice human sacrifice. The possibility that he, Chris, could become a celebrity by uncovering new evidence that would astound the world of archeology, was a dream come true.

As he continued to look around, he saw an opening in the far side of the cavern. As he stepped closer, he saw that a doorway ten feet high had been carved out of the rock, with an ornately carved archway serving as the entrance. It seemed so out of place with the rest of the cavern that he was at a loss of what to think. Stepping over to it and stooping down, he found a gold crucifix that had been placed there in a little wooden stand. Fascinated, he pulled the crucifix out of the stand, and examined it more closely. Its weight indicated that it was probably made of solid gold. By the design, and his knowledge of the history of the area, he assumed it was most likely of Spanish origin. He wondered if a group of Spanish missionaries had been sacrificed by the Indians.

He longed to continue his explorations, but glancing down at his watch he realized it was getting late, and that he needed to get back to the truck. The last thing he wanted was for Roger to come looking for him and find him here. Shoving the crucifix deep into his pack, he hastily made his way back through the various caves and tunnels to the main entrance on the mountainside.

As Chris emerged from the cave, he found a concerned Roger waiting for him by the four-wheel drive. "I was about to go in and start looking for you. I've never known you to be late for dinner before."

"Sorry. I lost track of time. I think maybe I'm getting close to the end of that tunnel, or at least I hope so. I'm going to give it one more day, and if I don't find anything, I'll give up."

"It's about time, Chris. You've already wasted too much time. For someone who professes to be as cool and logical as you do, you spend more wasted time on hunches than anyone I've ever met."

Chris was tempted to respond, but kept his peace. He didn't want to risk revealing anything to Roger in the heat of an argument.

They had decided to stay at the Humphries Inn, the hotel that had been established in the old Humphries' mansion over fifteen years ago. It was a very comfortable place to stay, and the accommodations were first class. After spending so much time in campsites at archeological digs that were miles away from civilization, the luxury of staying at a hotel was very greatly appreciated by both of them.

The next morning, Chris had once again made his way to the cavern. He had not been able to sleep at all the night before. Anticipation of his fame and success had him fantasizing all night long. He had hidden the crucifix with his personal belongings where he felt it should be safe from Roger's discovering it. He was convinced it was very valuable, and he wasn't about to turn it over to the university along with the other finds. The fact that the university was providing the funds for their explorations didn't concern Chris. He'd worked hard, and deserved a little extra.

Continuing where he'd left off the night before, he walked through the doorway. As he entered the chamber beyond, his wildest imaginings couldn't have prepared him for what he found. It was as if he had stepped into the entry hall of an ancient palace.

Everything was made of a rock he had never seen before. It was dark red in color, with streaks of black running through it, polished to a brilliant shine. The carvings on the walls were intricate and lifelike, and the greatest sculptures Chris had ever seen were put to shame. He was amazed at the imagination the creators of the hall must have had. All the carvings were nightmarish in their appearance. Depictions of beast-like human forms, gnarled and twisted, brought a shiver to Chris' spine despite his cool composure. Intertwined, the figures were all engaged in one large scene of mutual slaughter, with smiles of grim delight on their faces. A large ornately decorated pillar stood in the center of the hallway, and arched up into the ceiling. The arches continued through the ceiling and back down the walls, helping to form the various doorways that led from the room.

As Chris walked towards the pillar, he was surprised that the air around him seemed much colder than in the cavern. He also found himself becoming apprehensive. He shrugged off the feeling as being silly and reached out to touch the pillar. It was smooth as glass to the touch, but felt icy cold.

A soft laugh behind him caused him to spin around. Towering in front of him was a shadow that his light would not illuminate, chilling him to the bone. A quiet voice spoke from the shadow.

"Are you ready to receive your just rewards, my greedy little friend?"

Something lashed out at him, and he thought he could feel a momentary sting on his neck. Looking down, he cried out in horror as he saw his own blood flow down his chest.

In the back of his mind, Roger could have sworn he heard Chris cry out. Concerned for his impetuous colleague, he felt he should make certain Chris was all right. He found the tunnel Chris had been working on and made his way down it. Chris had obviously made a great deal more progress than what he had admitted to. Roger wondered what else Chris had elected to keep to himself. When Roger got to the end, he was surprised to find only the small opening at the ground. He called out to Chris through the opening, but heard no response. Getting on his hands and knees, he crawled through the opening. As he emerged from the tunnel, he was surprised that his light was swallowed up in the darkness in front of him. It was as if the light simply disappeared. It wasn't reflected back, it just ceased to exist when it hit the darkness. He looked up and saw a powerful arm with knotted muscles and dark red claws shining in the torchlight. Panicked, he tried to stand up, but hit his head on the rock ledge above him, and fell into darkness.

Chapter Two - Sunday Brunch

Father Randy gave the final blessing at the end of Mass, and prepared to exit the church in the recessional. He had been appointed as parochial vicar of this parish for a little over a year now, and at the age of thirty, was one of the younger priests in the diocese.

He surveyed the parishioners, and nodded to several of them as he walked down the aisle. He knew all of them quite well, and considered them his family. He had heard many critics of Catholicism assert that priests could not possibly understand families, since they had none of their own. How shortsighted of those critics, he thought. How many people in the world enjoyed a family of a thousand people? What a blessing to be a part of so many different cultures and societal levels.

As he reached the vestibule, he turned and stood to greet the parishioners as they came out of the church. This was always one of his favorite duties. He could briefly chat with everyone and catch little snippets of news that helped him keep up with the doings of the parish family.

He was pleasantly surprised to see who brought up the end of the line. "Mom, Dad," he exclaimed cheerfully. "It's always so wonderful to see you. And you brought Fred and Janet with you. That's great!"

Randy's parents had both turned gray over the intervening years. His mother had put on a little extra weight, and combined with her loss in height, she presented a much different appearance than during Randy's youth. His father retained his oversized stature and commanded the respect of all who knew him. Fred and Janet, much to the envy of all, had remained essentially unchanged. Except for a few small wrinkles around the eyes, the passage of the years had left them untouched.

He hugged each of them with a bear-like hug that left all of them breathless. Randy was not a small person. Six feet four inches tall and just under two hundred forty pounds in weight, he sometimes tended to underestimate his strength.

"Fred, Janet, where are the twins? Now that they've turned sixteen, I'm sure you're just chomping at the bit to teach them how to drive."

"Please, Randy," pleaded Janet, "don't remind him. Fred gets heart burn at the thought of his sweet precious girls going out by themselves."

"I doubt that they'll be going out by themselves very much." Randy had a broad grin stretched across his face. "They're both rather attractive, and I'm sure each one of them has boys standing in line to take them out on dates."

"Are you *trying* to ruin my day?" groaned Fred, pulling at his tie. "If so you're doing a wonderful job. I've already explained to both girls that they're still much too young to date, and I don't need you to stir things up."

"Oh come on, Fred." Janet sighed in exasperation. "You can't protect those girls forever. Sooner or later you've got to let go and let them learn to take care of themselves."

Fred put his arm around Janet's shoulders. "Later will do just fine. I assume that any boys those girls date will try the same things I did when I was that age. If they're lucky, I might let them start dating when they turn thirty."

"And just what things did you try?" Randy folded his arms and gave Fred an apprising look. "Is there something you'd like to confess?"

"I certainly wouldn't confess them to you," protested Fred. "I wouldn't want to tarnish the sterling image you have of me."

Janet laughed. "Randy, anytime you want to hear about the true Fred, just come to me. I won't go into any details now, but let me assure you, Fred's halo is anything but polished." She put her arms around Fred and continued. "Come to think of it, I'm not sure I would want him to be pure and innocent. He's a lot more fun the way he is."

"I'm shocked," quipped Randy. "Here you are pushing sixty, and you're acting like a bunch of teenage kids."

"Son, trust me," said Jake. "There's no reason to grow up before you have to. Your mother and I are putting it off as long as we can. Listen, since this is your last Mass of the day, we were hoping we could talk you into going to brunch with us. There's a new restaurant that opened up down the street that has an all-you-can-eat buffet."

"Sounds wonderful. I'm starved. Just give me a few minutes to get out of these vestments."

Ellen took Randy's hand. "Randy, before you run off, take these gladiolas I picked from the flower garden at home and put them in a vase of water. You can use them to brighten up your bedroom at the rectory."

"Thanks Mom, they're beautiful. I promise I'll take good care of them."

Randy hurried back into the church and went to the sacristy to take off his vestments and hang them up. He found a vase for the flowers in one of the cabinets, and left them in the sacristy for now. He figured he'd take them to the rectory when he got back. Even though he was happy to see his parents and good friends, he sensed that the visit was more than just social. Even though they all lived in the city now, it was rare to get everyone together at the same time. After selling the Humphries' house and their house, to the company that converted the property into a hotel, he and his parents had moved to Mesa Springs. The company that bought the property was all too happy to be able to buy both buildings. They felt that it was critical to their plans to reconvert Jake and Ellen's house back into the guesthouse for the hotel. They used it for VIPs that wanted a little extra privacy.

Jake and Ellen restarted their real estate careers after the move, and even though they were successful enough, the shadow of the past always seemed to hover over everything. Randy's nightmares took years to subside, and it wasn't until he started college that the horror of the experience had begun to fade. When he expressed to his parents his desire to enter the priesthood, they were at first concerned that he was doing so to hide from the past. It took many days of frank, heart-to-heart conversations to convince them that he had a true calling. His experiences certainly played a major part and caused him to sincerely question his beliefs; his turning to religion had been an outcome of that. But what started as an exploration into the world of faith resulted in an inner peace and a deep conviction that he had discovered his niche in life.

Fred pursued his relationship with Janet, and it wasn't long before they were married. Since Fred also became uncomfortable in Shady Valley, his decision to move into the city had come as no surprise. Janet was well established at the university, and it only seemed natural for her to retain her position there. Fred found a job with a local detective agency that paid considerably more than his job as sheriff had. When the twins were born, Janet took a couple of years off from her teaching duties, but soon went back in response to continued pleas from the university. With the various demands they all had on their time, it took a very important event to get them together.

After finishing up in the sacristy, Randy went back outside and they all piled into the big Lincoln Jake and Ellen used for their real estate business. They found that even though it was more fashionable to drive an upscale import, most clients still preferred the comfort of a large domestic luxury car.

Randy noticed that everyone was oddly quiet during the brief drive to the restaurant, and the trip through the buffet line. As always, Randy piled his plate as high as possible and sat down with enough food in front of him to feed an average person for a week.

"Okay everyone, what's up?" Randy wasn't going to wait any longer. "You know I love to see all of you, but I suspect there's more to this visit than you've let on." He voraciously dug into his plate.

"As always, you're very observant," admitted Jake, while buttering a roll. "And you know what? It's a shame that you're right. It shouldn't take a crisis to get us all together. I suppose it's an unfortunate sign of the times we live in. Your mother and I are always talking about trying to slow things down, but it seems like every time we try, it just gets worse." Jake paused to take a bite out of the roll before continuing. "However, getting back to the reason for our visit, I'm sure you probably heard about the two archeologists that got lost in the caves in Shady Valley. They still haven't been found."

"Of course I've heard. But what of it? Those caves are a real maze, and nobody knows how far back they go. It wouldn't be terribly difficult for someone to get lost in them. Not only that, but if the demon were on the loose, I suspect we would have had far more chilling news stories than just two missing archeologists."

"Maybe," replied Jake skeptically. "I'm not so sure. If I were the demon, I'm not certain I'd want to attract a lot of attention. The demon might be immortal, but a herd of reporters would be enough to make anything's existence miserable. We just wanted to make sure you weren't planning anything foolish. I doubt that that clerical collar of yours would make you immune. And as far as any special powers are concerned, let's be honest son. No one has ever seen any evidence of your being any different than anyone else. We don't want to see you go charging off and getting yourself killed just because you think it's your destiny."

For years after the incident, Randy could not get the image of the demon out of his mind. Its words to him, *You and I are destined to meet again Randy*, were forever imprinted into his memory. As he became older, and studied theology more deeply, he realized that the forces of evil delighted in fabrications designed to torment people. He eventually learned to lead his life free of any supposed destiny. As far as any special powers were concerned, there again, the conversation between Rachel and the demon was difficult to forget. As a teenager, he had tried to explore whether or not he had any powers. He tried to move objects with his mind, read other people's thoughts, and so on. All of his efforts were fruitless. In particular, he remembered one disastrous attempt to control his girl friend's mind while on a date. The only reward he got for his effort was a slap across the face. No, he thought to himself, he wasn't any different. If the demon thought so, that was its mistake.

"Dad, do you really think I'd just take off on my own without talking to you guys first?

"Yes," protested Fred, "absolutely. It certainly wouldn't be the first time you broke your promise to me to stay out of trouble."

"Listen everyone. I'm not going to lie to you. If I thought people's lives were in danger, and there was even the remotest possibility of my helping, I'd be there in a heartbeat. But so far, nothing has occurred to make me suspect that the demon is on the loose. We all helped seal up the various entryways into the passages. If anyone released the demon, it would have to have been through those passageways. There were no other caves connecting into those passageways. The archeologists were exploring the existing caves in the valley, not tearing apart the Humphries house. Besides, since the Humphries house is now a state landmark, no one can ever tear it apart. It has to be preserved in its present condition. It's going to take more than a couple of lost archeologists to make me think the demon's terrorizing Shady Valley."

Randy turned his attention back to the plate of food in front of him, acting as though everything were perfectly normal, despite the sudden hush that had fallen over the group. He hoped no one would notice the slight shaking of his fork as he carefully brought each bite of food to his mouth.

Chapter Three - Monday

The next day, Randy had just finished a mid-afternoon meeting with a couple seeking to get married in the church, when he decided to raid the kitchen in the rectory for a snack. The housekeeper was used to having Randy come in looking for food, and liked to have something ready for him if she could. Today, she had some fresh strawberries all washed and ready to eat sitting in a bowl on the kitchen table. The housekeeper, Betty, was an elderly widow whose own children had long since moved away, and she enjoyed mothering the priests of the parish.

When Randy walked in, she was working at the counter that divided the kitchen from the eating space, trying to cut a chicken in half that wasn't quite defrosted yet. Even though the butcher knife was sharp, she was having a great deal of difficulty getting it through the icy chicken. In sudden exasperation, she raised the knife above her head to chop it into the chicken with all her strength. Just as Randy stepped in front of her, she brought the knife down as hard as she could. Much to her surprise and horror, the blade came loose from the handle, and shot towards Randy's chest. With a sickening thud, it struck him.

"My God, what have I done!" Betty put her hands to her cheeks in horror. In shock, she dropped the knife handle and collapsed to the floor. When she came to, she was still on the floor, but Randy was stooped next to her, cradling her head. She took a deep breath and tried to regain her thoughts. As full recollection flooded back into her, her eyes opened wide in disbelief.

"Father, I don't understand," Betty stammered. "I saw the knife go into your chest."

Quietly, Randy picked up the large wooden cross that he always wore. Embedded in the center was the knife blade. "I'm glad you have excellent aim. Just a fraction of an inch to either side, and I think St. Peter and I would now be getting to know one and another. Are *you* all right? You took a nasty fall."

"I'll be just fine, Father." Her voice wavered as she shook. "But I still don't understand what happened."

"Well," said Randy slowly as he studied the knife blade, "it appears that they don't make things the way they used to. Just look. There was only about an inch of metal for the plastic handle to hold on to. It must have come loose just in time for you to start your career in knife throwing."

"Father, please don't joke about it." With Randy's help, she got to her feet. "I feel badly enough as it is. I realize that you're always making light of everything, but I can't get out of my mind the thought that I almost killed you, and would have, if the good Lord hadn't helped."

"Well, let this be a lesson to the both of us. Everything happens in God's time, and not before. It wasn't time for me to go yet, and it wasn't time for you to change careers yet. You're not done fattening me up. Now, get me a more reliable knife and I'll cut up this chicken for you, if you show me what you've got for my snack."

After eating the strawberries, and spending some time chatting with Betty, Randy felt more refreshed, and a little calmer. He didn't want to upset Betty any more than she already was, so he put on a brave face and pretended that the entire affair was nothing to fret over. In reality, he was somewhat shaken up himself.

He stepped out on the back porch of the rectory to get away from the heat Betty was starting to create in the kitchen with her cooking. The back porch was one of his favorite places to relax. The rectory was an older house, probably somewhere between fifty and seventy years old. The backyard had two very large, mature trees that provided shade, and helped provide a peaceful environment. Randy enjoyed sitting on the porch, and listening to the wind chimes that provided soft music in the breeze.

Randy took a couple of steps, slipped, and felt his feet go right out from under him. His feet knocked out one of the posts supporting the roof, and the whole roof caved in on top of him. He could hear the sound of Betty screaming frantically for help.

Hearing all the commotion, Father Joe, the elderly pastor, came running into the kitchen. He hurried to Betty to find out what was wrong. He took her shoulders in his hands, and turned her towards him.

"Betty, please try to calm down," he said as steadily as he could. "Tell me what's wrong."

"The roof fell on Father Randy." she pointed towards the back window.

Full of alarm, Joe grabbed for the telephone and dialed 911 for help. After making sure help was on its way, he ran out of the front of the house and around to the back to see if there was anything he could do. The roof seemed to have come straight down, but try as he might, he could not budge any part of it. He called out, and was rewarded with hearing a muffled answer.

"I'm okay, but I'm trapped and can't get out."

"Hold on! Help is on its way."

When the emergency crew arrived, it took a great deal of effort to get the roof off of Randy. It was too heavy to move, and they ended up cutting away a section of it in order to get Randy out. Except for a few bruises, Randy seemed to be no worse for the experience. Since he was already down when the roof fell, he had not received any blows. The ceiling of the roof was somewhat recessed. Even though it held him in place, he was not crushed. Betty was a different story. She was so upset, they ended up giving her tranquilizers and having someone take her home.

Later that evening Randy and Joe were surveying the damage, and both of them were amazed at the extent. The porch roof had sheared away from the house, and taken some of the siding with it. Most of the porch itself was also beyond repair, having been crushed by the weight of the roof coming down.

"Randy, your guardian angel sure worked hard today." Joe shook his head. "Barely escaping that knife this afternoon was miraculous enough, but walking away from this mess unharmed, defies the imagination. I hope your not planning on doing any encores. I'm not sure the parish could afford the damage, not to mention the toll all of this is taking on my nerves. I don't think my hair could get any whiter, but I'd at least like to keep what little of it I have left."

Randy affectionately put his arm around the slender man. "Believe me Joe, if I had realized what was going to happen to me today, I would have stayed in bed. I've had bad Mondays before, but this is ridiculous. You'd think someone up there was trying to tell me something. I think I'm going to have a strong drink tonight, and turn in as early as possible. I don't want to tempt fate by staying up any longer than necessary."

True to his word, Randy enjoyed a couple of Black Russians, his favorite drink, and was in bed by 10:30. He always liked to read before he went to sleep, but found that the drinks made concentration a little more challenging than usual. He tried stubbornly for about ten minutes, but finally gave up and turned out the lights. He fell asleep quickly. It had been a particularly hot day, and his cool bedroom was especially relaxing. He had chosen the basement bedroom for that very reason. Even though the rectory was not air-conditioned, the basement always stayed very cool and comfortable all summer.

It was just before midnight when there was a soft rustling of the curtains. Randy had fallen into a particularly deep sleep, and was not awakened by the soft sound of something falling from the window to the floor. A large rattlesnake had crawled through a hole in the screen and was quietly surveying the surroundings. Attracted by the sounds of Randy's soft snoring, it slowly slithered to the bed. It was extremely large for a rattlesnake, well over ten feet in length, and had a strange appearance to it. Almost red in color, it had an eerie, phosphorescent glow. The eyes, in particular, were like two dark-red, shining embers. When it reached the bed, it raised its head somewhat, and moved its neck back and forth, studying the bed.

Suddenly, Randy turned over in his sleep, and one of his arms was flung over the side of the bed. His hand hit the snake right on the head. Startled, the snake darted back and stared at the hand with malice building in its eyes. It shook its tail, but the rattle wasn't enough to wake Randy. The snake opened its mouth, baring its venomous fangs. The snake's mouth gleamed with spittle, and it hissed in anger. Slowly, it gathered its coils together to strike at the hand which dangled in front of it. Quickly it lunged at Randy's hand, but missed. Once again, Randy had turned in his sleep, and pulled his hand out of harm's way at the last instant. Enraged, the snake crawled to the foot of the bed, and began to make its way up one of the legs. Slowly it climbed up to the bed, and regarded the sleeping form of Randy. It slithered over the covers to the pillow, and stopped just inches from Randy's face. Again, it shook its tail in anger.

This time, Randy woke up. Opening his eyes, he saw the snake bearing its fangs at him. Purely out of reflex, he rolled away from the snake and turned the pillow over on the snake's head. Jumping out of bed, he ran towards the light switch and turned on the room's two lamps. Looking towards the bed, he saw that the snake was gone. He heard noises of its moving around, but couldn't figure out where they were coming from. He started to move along the wall towards the door, when the snake crawled out from behind the dresser just a few feet away from him. He had seen enough rattlers in action in the mountains, and knew he'd never make it to the door. He couldn't imagine how this one had gotten so far into the city, much less bother to enter the house, but he didn't waste any thought on the mystery.

He looked around the room in vain for something he could use as a weapon. Once again the snake began to gather its coils, and Randy knew he didn't have much time left. Out of the corner of his eye, he saw the vase of flowers that his mother had given him, and acted immediately on an idea that popped into his head. He grabbed the vase and threw the flowers and water on the snake. The snake hissed in anger and started towards Randy. Randy then picked up the lamp next to him. Ripping away the shade, he threw it light bulb first into the puddle of water around the snake. The resultant flash blinded him and the room was plunged into darkness as the circuit breaker was tripped.

Randy ran over to the closet and flung the door open, reaching for the flashlight that he always kept on the top shelf. He turned it on, and with his hand shaking, shone it over to where the snake was. The snake appeared to be lifeless and just lay in the water. He threw a coat hanger at it, but it remained motionless. Breathing a little easier, he reached into the closet behind him for the hunting knife that hung in its sheath from one of the coat hooks. Not taking his eyes from the snake, he fumbled with his one free hand trying to unlatch the sheath's clasp. Snapping it free, he pulled the knife out, and walked towards the door. Remaining cautious, he moved very slowly, carefully taking each step. As he approached the snake, he stepped into the water that had spread across the floor. Suddenly, he saw the snake's eyes light up. Quick as lightening it thrust towards him. Trying to jump out of its way, Randy slipped on the wet floor, and fell towards the snake. In desperation, he struck out with his knife on the way down. When he hit the floor he rolled away as quickly as he could and turned to see where the snake was.

Once again, his guardian angel had intervened. When he fell and struck out with his knife, he managed to land in such a way that the knife severed the head from the snake. It now lay dead, the body still twitching.

Shaking, Randy picked the broken lamp off the floor and unplugged it. Using his flashlight, he made his way to the breaker panel on the back of the house and reset the circuit breaker. He returned to his room and started to clean up the mess. He picked up the snake's head to look more closely at it. He had realized from the start that this was no ordinary rattlesnake. He opened its mouth, and looked at the fangs. Instead of being white, the fangs were a deep blood red in color. The same color as Rachel's claws when she was in her demon form. He dropped the head in shock, and then stared in horror as the entire snake dissolved in smoke before his eyes.

Chapter Four - The Humphries Inn

Despite the hot afternoon sun, Randy couldn't suppress a shiver when he walked up the steps of the Humphries Inn. Seeing the old house again brought back the memories as sharp and clear as though the entire affair had taken place last week, rather than eighteen years ago. His hand went to his cheek and lightly touched the faint scar that was still there. Since the time Randy and his parents moved away from Shady Valley, Randy had not returned. He always tried to put the incident behind him, and hoped this day would never come.

He walked into the lobby of the hotel, and observed that the house had been kept as intact as possible. A large desk was constructed against one of the walls of the entry hall to serve as the front desk, but otherwise the hall remained unchanged. Looking from side to side, he saw that the living room was now a formal dining area, and that the library was converted into a coffee shop. He was glad to see, however, that the character of the two rooms remained the same. The library retained all of its shelves, which were filled with a variety of books in order to create the proper atmosphere.

He walked to the front desk to register. He had called in the morning to make a reservation, and to make certain it would be on the second floor. The second floor was the only one with complete access to the secret passageways honeycombing the house. He hoped that in the process of remodeling, no one had inadvertently discovered any of the secret panels opening into the passageways. He would soon find out.

Even though he didn't tell Joe about the rattlesnake in his room last night, getting a couple of days off had been easy. In light of the previous day's accidents, Joe could very well understand Randy's desire to unwind for awhile.

As he was filling out the registration card, he couldn't help but overhear the manager talking to an elderly couple at the end of the desk.

"If you hear any strange noises during the night, just disregard them." The thin, balding man was adjusting his tie. "Late at night, the ghost of Rachel Humphries sometimes walks the halls. Rachel was missing after the gruesome murder of one of the servants more than sixty years ago, and has never been seen or heard from since." The manager paused for effect while he brushed back the few stands of hair that still remained on top of his head. "Even though no one will confirm it, *I* believe that Rachel also came to a grizzly untimely end, which is why her spirit haunts the house. You needn't worry, however. When I've seen her walk the halls, she's always looked sad and lonely, incapable of harming anyone."

Randy almost choked on that last comment. The couple seemed impressed however, and walked away with looks of awe in their eyes. As the manager turned around, Randy could have sworn he muttered "gullible fools" under his breath.

His curiosity aroused, Randy tried to get the manager's attention. "Excuse me, sir. I see by your name tag that you're the manager."

"Yes sir, Winston Chamberlain at your service," the manager replied in a huffy autocratic tone, his mustache quivering on his thin upper lip. "How may I be of assistance?"

"I couldn't help but overhear what you said to that couple just now. I take it that you've been managing the property for some time now, since you've seen the ghost so often."

"Yes sir. I'm also part owner, and live on the premises in what used to be the master bedroom suite."

"I'm surprised you didn't decide to live in the old guest house. My parents and I used to live there until it was sold eighteen years ago. I would think it would be much more comfortable."

"Oh my, I could never afford to do that. The guest house is reserved for dignitaries only and costs more than a thousand dollars per day."

"Wow. At that price I wouldn't think you'd have much interest for it here in Shady Valley."

"On the contrary, it's occupied most of the time. It just happens to be vacant this week."

"Well thank you for satisfying my curiosity, Mr. Chamberlain. I'm looking forward to my visit here."

"If there's anything I can do for you sir, please feel free to call on me." He brushed a small piece of lint from his neatly pressed black suit.

Randy had to choke down a chuckle at the manager's haughty tone, and hoped that the rest of the hotel employees were not of the same mold.

The desk clerk offered to take Randy's bag up to his room for him, but Randy declined. He had packed light since he was only planning on spending a couple of days. He assumed the matter would be resolved quickly one way or another. He did not delude himself into believing that his chances of survival were anything but slim.

He found his room easily enough at the end of the second floor hallway. The room was comfortably furnished in a style that was in keeping with the age of the house. A king-size four-post bed dominated the room. The dresser, with the large oval mirror, was finished in antique white. An overstuffed chair was placed close to the window where a clear view of the grounds could be enjoyed. Here again, the room had not been remodeled, but kept as original as possible. If the purpose of his trip were not so dire, he would very much enjoy his stay here.

After unpacking his bag, Randy took out the tools he had brought with him and went to work. The secret panels in the bedrooms were all in the dressing rooms, and were activated by pulling on one of the coat hooks. Randy remembered precisely how he and his father had disabled them, and came prepared with the appropriate tools.

He unscrewed the coat hook that used to be the trigger. Removing it, he found the small hole that he expected. He took the steel rod he had fashioned with the hook on the end. Carefully, he inserted the steel rod, hook first, through the hole. He fumbled around a bit, but was soon rewarded by catching the trip wire he knew would be there. With a sharp tug, he released the panel's locks. Creaking from misuse, the panel opened to reveal the passageway behind it. A musty odor flowed out of it followed by a cloud of dust. Randy coughed, and waited for the air to clear.

Switching on the heavy-duty lamp he brought with him, he looked into the passageway. A thick layer of dust covered everything, including the floor. It was obvious that nothing had been in there for years.

Gingerly he stepped in, and started towards the center of the house. Making his way down the passageway, he suppressed the urge to check out the rooms he passed. There was a small panel that could be slid aside to expose a small peep hole, but he reasoned that what was going on in those rooms was none of his business.

He soon came to the narrow staircase at the end and proceeded down as softly as possible. The last thing he wanted to do was make a lot of noise and alert someone in the hotel of his presence inside the walls. He passed the branch that went up to the master bedroom, and smiled as an idea came to him. If the opportunity arose, he thought, he just might act on it.

Eventually, he came to Rachel's secret library, well under the house. Here again, the dust was testimony to the fact that nothing had disturbed the chamber. The sense of evil that permeated the place had not diminished over the years, however. Randy absent-mindedly fingered the crucifix that hung around his neck in order to reassure himself.

He stepped over to the book shelves and became chilled with dread as he scanned some of the titles: *The Secret Rites of Demonology*; *The History of Witchcraft*; *Ritual Sacrifice - The Key to Power*; *Secrets of the Black Arts*; *Ancient Black Mythology*; *The Sorcerer's Handbook*; *Society of the Dagger and Scorpion - Member's Handbook*; and so on. After reading all that, he thought, it was no wonder Rachel began to lose her sanity. The only title he found missing was *Witchcraft for Dummies*.

The massive wooden door that led to Rachel's cage was still ajar, and he was able to squeeze through the opening. Illuminating the interior, he was still amazed at how Humphries could have kept his mother locked up like some wild animal for all those years. Randy just couldn't imagine how father and son could have rationalized their cruel imprisonment of a human being, no matter what the circumstances. Even after the incident was over, Humphries was never able to get over it and find peace. Years later he committed suicide by slitting his own throat with a knife. Randy remembered his surprise fifteen years ago when he received a package in the mail from Humphries. Inside it he had found Humphries' St. Michael medallion along with a short note.

> Randy, enclosed you will find my St. Michael medallion. I have no further need of it. Fr. Brian told me that if it weren't for you, I would not have gotten it back. I am deeply sorry for all you went through because of my family. I hope this medallion will help you in the future.

Stepping into the cage, he saw the picture of Rachel Humphries still lying on the desk. Picking it up, he looked at the picture, and a tear came to his eyes as he realized the torture the poor woman must have gone through. He had long since learned to forgive Rachel, realizing that her part in the tragedy was mostly a result of Gorshault's influence. He prayed often for God's forgiveness and mercy for her.

He went back into the passageway, and continued his initial exploration. It wasn't long before he came to the cave, and turned into it. He became as careful as possible, and walked quietly. He finally found evidence that someone had been there, when he found the arrow that had been painted on the cave wall. Shining his light at it, he found the opening under the ledge. He realized how they all could have walked right past it without seeing it all those years ago. Looking down, he saw brown stains on the floor, and realized it was very likely that blood had been spilled there recently.

Taking a deep breath, he continued onward until he came to the chamber. His memories of it were not clear, since he had been brought there by Rachel while still unconscious. He hadn't come to until shortly before Fred and his father arrived. The battle that followed afterwards happened so quickly that Randy had not had any time to study the chamber.

He saw with alarm that the cave-in had been partially cleared away. Taking a deep breath, he slowly stepped in and looked around. Ignoring everything else, Randy found his attention focused on one thing. Looking towards the entrance to Gorshault's abode, he saw that the crucifix was gone and that his worst fears had been realized. Gorshault was free.

Chapter Five - The Diary

Randy was not ready to face the demon yet, and needed a little time to prepare himself mentally and emotionally for the encounter.

He went back to Rachel's library in the hopes of finding something that would help him. Rachel's leather bound diary was still on the table, a thick layer of dust and cobwebs draped over it. Deciding it might be his best source of information, Randy set his lamp next to it and sat down. He sneezed as he opened it and the dust rose up around him. The sound of his sneeze echoed off the hard stone walls.

He found that she had begun her diary with her arrival at the mansion. From the earliest passages on, her loneliness became very apparent, and was compounded by the fact that she appeared to be a passionate woman. Randy blushed somewhat when reading through some of the passages, and felt very uncomfortable. The vow of celibacy was not an easy restriction for a healthy, thirty-year-old priest to deal with.

He continued to scan through until he came to the passage he was looking for.

Dear diary, today I found a fascinating manuscript that seems to be the diary of a Spanish missionary priest that came through this valley hundreds of years ago. It talks of a demon that's trapped in a cave somewhere in the valley. I wonder how my father-in-law came across it. The only conclusion I can come up with is that he found it while digging the various passageways under the house. I went through them very carefully today, and found a section in the one going to the guesthouse, where the bricks didn't quite match. I pounded on it with a hammer, and it sounded hollow. I don't think I'm strong enough to break it down myself, but I'll ask Steven to help. He gets bored with the gardening, and from the way he looks at me, I think he'll do anything I ask.

Randy shifted in the chair, trying to make himself more comfortable. The next entry was not what he expected.

Dear diary, my underground explorations will have to wait. I am now convinced that what I have suspected for some weeks is definitely true. I'm pregnant. I have so many preparations to make. I only hope that a child will help keep Joseph home more often.

From that point on, the diary spoke of nothing but Rachel's pregnancy, and then later, her life as mother of Joey, her son. From what Randy could see, she loved her son dearly, and was very close to him. Contrary to her hopes, her husband had not spent more time at home, leaving the entire task of raising Joey to Rachel. Randy flipped through pages and pages before he once again found the entries he was looking for.

>   Dear diary, my life seems so empty now that Joey's gone to college. I've been getting so bored. This morning I remembered the Spanish diary I found before Joey was born. It seems so long ago, that I almost think it was in another lifetime. I had Steven start to break down the bricked off section of the passageway. He was only too happy to help, and I'm sure he'll keep it secret. His reaction to my light touch on his arm, and the smile I gave him, convinces me he'll do whatever I want.

>   Dear diary, Steven removed the last of the section of the wall that blocked off the cave I just knew I would find. We followed the cave into the mountain and came to a cavern filled with skeletons. At the far end was the cave-in with the skeleton of the missionary priest still partially trapped underneath. I put Steven to work with explicit instructions to remove only the rocks themselves, nothing else. He seemed a little reluctant to work with all those skeletons lying around, but when I gave him a little kiss on the cheek, he became dazed and went right to work.

>   Dear diary, Steven's been working on removing the cave-in for two days now. Some

of the rocks are so heavy that I've been helping him. I have to admit, he's not very talkative, but he is likable, and it's kind of fun to flirt with him while we're working together.

Dear diary, we started to break through this morning, and I could see the reddish glow of the demon's underground palace filtering through the rocks. Since all the large rocks seemed to be removed, I thanked Steven for his help and told him I could finish up. He seemed reluctant to leave, but after I gave him a big hug for his help, he agreed to go back to his gardening. I told him in a husky voice that I hoped we could continue to get to know one another better, and he left with a broad smile on his face. I'm sure I'll be able to talk him into helping whenever I need to. It took me the rest of the day to clear out the remaining rocks, and it was harder than I thought it would be, but I couldn't risk Steven seeing what was beyond the cave-in. It was late night before the last rock was rolled away, and I came across the crucifix in its little wooden stand. Needless to say, I left it in place. I looked around it as well as I could, but could not find any sign of the supposed demon. I wonder if he really exists, or if he was just a figment of the imagination of a dying priest.

Dear diary, when I went down to the cavern this morning, the demon was waiting for me on the other side of the crucifix. At first I was terrified, but he spoke to me and we had a long conversation together. I can't say what he looks like. All I can see is a large shadow. His name is Gorshault, and he denies being a demon. He says he is an immortal being, and is above the concept of good and evil. He constructed his underground palace here centuries ago, just before humans started arriving from the north. When I asked him why the crucifix kept him trapped, he grew angry and left.

Dear diary, Gorshault was waiting for me in the morning again, and we continued our conversation. He apologized for growing angry. He said that the crucifix is a symbol of a rival power, nothing more. He said again that the concept of good and evil is meaningless, and that each power wished to do the same thing. Bring order to the world. He said that the only differences between the powers were the methods used. When I explained to him that evil preys on people's fears, he responded by saying that religion does the same thing, by threatening you with eternal damnation if you're not good. It's obvious I need to do more research. I told Gorshault that I would be taking a long trip, and wouldn't be down to see him for awhile. That will give me the time I need to contact Joey and have him get me some books on the occult so I'll be better prepared the next time I meet Gorshault.

Randy again skipped through several more entries that spoke of Rachel's research into the subject of demonology and witchcraft. It seemed that all her studying was for naught as far as understanding Gorshault was concerned. Rachel grew more and more intrigued with the actual satanic rituals themselves, and the power they promised to provide. It wasn't long before her emphasis shifted to the search for eternal life. From the various entries he had read, it was obvious that Rachel had always been somewhat obsessed with her appearance, and many of the books promised eternal beauty. Soon, she went back to Gorshault, not with the purpose of better understanding what he was, but to seek his help in the workings of the various rituals she had read about. Gorshault was only too happy to assist. Little by little he was able to feed her hunger for power, and twist her into a creature of his own molding. She did seem to retain one small shred of common sense, in that she refused to remove the crucifix for him. Even though she wouldn't admit it to Gorshault, it wasn't long before she herself began to fear it. After time, she couldn't have touched it even if she wished. Randy came across one entry in particular that caught his attention.

> Dear diary, it appears that the mighty Gorshault himself is not without fear. He spoke today of seeing someone in his future who might possibly destroy him. Being immortal, he did not know how this was to be accomplished, but only said that his existence, as he knew it, could come to an end.

Randy began to formulate an idea on how to approach Gorshault. He continued to scan the diary to see if he could find any other useful information.

Rachel did indeed gain substantial powers. For one thing, she eventually learned to change her shape to become either a beast-like creature with incredible physical strength, or to take on the shape and voice of other human beings. This explained to Randy her ability to appear as his six-year-old cousin when she eventually kidnapped him.

Before long, Rachel began to tire of performing minor rituals, and expressed her desire to Gorshault to move on to a higher level. He convinced her that the only way for her to progress, would be to perform a human sacrifice.

> Dear diary, I need to build an altar for my sacrificial ritual, as per the instructions that Gorshault has given me. He says that the human sacrifice will allow me to substantially lengthen my life, and I can hardly wait to proceed. As always, I have called on Steven to help me. Gorshault is staying out of view as Steven works on the altar for me. As long as I wear revealing outfits, and hint to him of the possibility of a romantic encounter together, he blindly does everything I ask of him. Little does he know that he is helping to construct the scene of his own death. His wish will indeed be granted, and we will be joined."

Randy had read enough. Even though the information he learned about Gorshault was not extensive, it was enough to give him an idea of how to proceed.

Chapter Six - The Tree House

As Randy began to stand up, he noticed a small drawer underneath the table. Opening it, he found some stationary in it with the name of Rachel Humphries embossed on it. It was somewhat yellowed with age, but still usable. Next to it were an old pen along with a bottle of ink that had been sealed well enough to keep it from drying up. Smiling mischievously to himself, he took out the pen and paper, and as carefully as he could, tried to emulate Rachel's flowing script.

> My Dearest Winston,
>   I have watched you for many years now, and my passion for you has become more than I can bear. I long to feel your arms around me, holding me in your firm embrace. I will come for you later, and take you with me to the hereafter, where we can be together for all eternity.
>   With Deepest Love, Rachel

He folded the letter and put it in his pocket. He then went back to the cage Rachel had been kept in, and looked through the chest of drawers for something appropriate for his plan. Finding it, he gingerly folded it, and took it with him.

This time, when he came to the fork in the staircase, he took the left-hand branch to the master bedroom suite, now the manager's apartment. When he got to the panel, he opened the little cover to the peephole and looked in to see if he could find Mr. Chamberlain anywhere. Not seeing or hearing anything, he cautiously opened the panel, and stepped into the room. He carefully checked everywhere, and concluded that Mr. Chamberlain was definitely not there. He took the note and left it on the pillow of the bed. He hastened to leave, and was glad he did. As soon as he closed the panel behind him, he heard the door to the bedroom open. Looking through the peephole, he saw Mr. Chamberlain come into the room, and walk over to the television to turn it on. He turned to go into the bathroom, when he spied the note on his bed. Picking it up, he read it. Mumbling something angrily under his breath, he crumpled it up and threw it into the trash can. Randy smiled to himself. Step one was successful.

He went back to his room and changed out of his dusty clothes. After he dressed, he carefully took his crucifix and put it inside his shirt. Very often, he preferred not to announce his being a priest. People around him were more relaxed that way. He headed to the dining room hoping it wasn't too late to get something to eat. It was 9:30, and indeed the dining room had closed, but the coffee shop was still open. He felt conspicuous as the only customer there, but he was famished. The waitress was an attractive brunette in her mid-twenties. After taking his order, she turned it in to the kitchen. She came back with his steak just a short time later. Needing some information, Randy started a conversation with her.

"Excuse me, I noticed when I came downstairs that Mr. Chamberlain, the manager, was nowhere to be seen. Is he still on the property?'

"Oh sure. He just goes to bed real early. He's one of them early risers. He's probably sound asleep by now."

Randy hoped that the stuffy manager had something more on his mind that might make his sleep a little less than sound. However, finding out that Mr. Chamberlain was an early sleeper, Randy had discovered what he wanted. He started to eat his dinner, but the waitress continued the conversation.

"So what brings you to Shady Valley?" She leaned against the chair across the table from him. "Are you on vacation, or travelin' for business?"

"Just taking a little rest," he answered as curtly as possible, hoping she would let him eat in peace.

"Sure wish I could take a rest," she said wistfully, her fingers twirling her pencil. "But I got to work all the time now. My live-in boyfriend ain't workin' right now, so I got to make lots of money so's I can pay the bills. I probably should'a thought of that before I let him move in. But ya know? It's kind'a nice to have a warm body to keep ya company at night. Know what I mean?" She gave him a sly wink.

"No, I'm sorry I wouldn't, Miss, I'm a priest."

"Oh, sorry to bother ya." She hastily hurried off.

Randy smiled to himself. At least now he'd be able to eat his dinner in peace.

Randy ate slowly, hoping to kill a little time. After dinner, it was well past 10:00, and he hoped the indubitable Mr. Chamberlain would be asleep enough for Randy to complete his prank. He went back to his room and grabbed the white nightgown he had taken from Rachel's chest of drawers, a clothes hanger, the long rod, and the hook he had brought with him to open the panel with. Being careful not to get the nightgown dusty, he went through the passageways back to the master bedroom suite. Looking through the peephole again, he saw that the manager appeared to be well asleep. The sounds of his soft snoring filled the room. Quietly, Randy opened the panel and crept into the room to the foot of the bed. He crouched down, and put the nightgown on the clothes hanger. Putting the hanger on the rod and hook assembly, he hoisted it up as high as he could reach. Then making his voice as high pitched as possible, went, "Oooooooooooooo," while at the same time shaking the bed.

The manager sat rigidly up in bed, took one look at the apparition that appeared to hover over his bed, and screamed.

"No, no, I'm not ready to go yet. Leave me alone." He jumped out of bed, and ran out the door screaming.

"Gullible fool," Randy chuckled to himself. Ah well, he thought, another practical joke he'd have to confess to Father Joe.

Randy quickly gathered everything, and made his way back to his room. Putting it away, he left his room, went downstairs, and walked up to the desk clerk.

"Excuse me. I could have sworn I heard some screaming. Is everything all right?'

"I don't know." The desk clerk's eyebrows were raised in question. "Mr. Chamberlain, the manager, just came running though here in his pajamas screaming 'You can't have me,' then ran out of the building. I'm concerned for him, but I don't know what to do."

"Well, I was going to step outside myself for a little night air. If I see him, I'll be sure to express your concern to him."

"Oh, thank you sir, that would be very helpful."

Still chuckling to himself, Randy stepped outside on the porch. It was a beautiful night. The stars shone brightly overhead, and there was just a slight breeze to help cool everything down from the day's heat that still lingered. He wandered about, not paying any attention to where he was headed. He wanted to enjoy this last night before he had to face Gorshault in the morning. His prank on Mr. Chamberlain had been an attempt to distract himself from the dire situation he was in. He tried to put all thoughts of the upcoming encounter out of his mind, focusing instead on the pleasant boyhood memories he had of Shady Valley.

He was pleased to see that the grounds were being immaculately tended to. As he walked through the trees, he came to a walled off area that he remembered was the Humphries' family cemetery. The vines clinging to the walls had been nicely tended to with flowers growing on them. The spider webs were all removed. He went to the gate and stepped inside. He was happy to see that the cemetery also was well maintained. Beautiful gardens had been planted throughout, and the gazebo was completely restored. The gravestones were neatly cleaned with the lettering sharply defined in the moonlight. He wished he had come here in the daylight so that he could have enjoyed the flowers.

Leaving the cemetery, he walked over to his old house. He was glad he knew it wasn't occupied right now. He would be able to wander around without fear of disturbing anyone. He stepped through the gate in the fence that still separated the guesthouse's yard from the mansion's grounds. Except for having a more manicured appearance to it, the yard looked essentially the same as when he last saw it.

He walked over to the tree where he had sat with Thunder so often on warm summer days, confiding to him all of his hopes and wishes. The memories brought tears to his eyes. Just over by the fence, was the grave they had dug for Thunder. Shortly after killing Rachel, he had gotten mysteriously sick. No matter what the veterinarian had tried, nothing seemed to help. The large dog had gotten progressively weaker as the days went by, until one day, while Randy was holding Thunder's big head in his lap, the faithful animal breathed his last. Randy wept quietly as he remembered that day. He helped his father dig the grave, and cried as they lowered Thunder's body into it. The sounds of the dirt that fell on Thunder's body still echoed in Randy's ears. Randy believed that one day, when he finally went to heaven, Thunder would be waiting for him. He was convinced that the St. Bernard's loyalty would transcend death.

Randy glanced upwards, and was amazed to see that the tree house he and his father built was still there. He was sure they would have taken it down for reasons of liability, in case one of the guests climbed up there and got hurt. The rope ladder that once provided access had been removed, but that wouldn't stop someone who was determined thought Randy. As a matter of fact, it wasn't going to stop him either. Jumping up, he grabbed one of the lower branches and swung himself into the tree. He only had to climb up a short distance to get to the door. It opened easily enough, and he crawled in. Even though it had once been thoroughly painted, eighteen years had taken its toll. The paint was starting to peel, and some of the boards were beginning to warp. All in all though, the interior was in fairly good shape, and the structure still had a solid feel to it. On sudden inspiration, Randy opened the cabinet that was built into one of the window seats. He was delighted to find the sleeping bag that he had always kept there. It was tightly wrapped in plastic, and seemed to be no worse for the wear. He had put it there as a boy, so that he could occasionally sneak out of the house after dark and spend the night there without having to tell his parents. Randy unrolled the bag, and lay down in it. It was a little too small for him, but his memories made it the most comfortable bed he could remember. Thinking of the times he had spent in the tree house, he slowly fell asleep, and slept better than he had in eighteen years.

Chapter Seven - Gorshault

Randy was surprised when he woke up in the tree house the next morning. He had not planned to spend the night there, but decided he was glad he did. He felt more refreshed than he had in a long time. He almost felt ready to face Gorshault. But, ready or not, he no longer had any choice. It had to be done today, regardless of the outcome.

He hurried back to the hotel and went to his room so he could prepare himself. When he arrived there, he was glad that he had spent the night in the tree house. The panel into the passageways stood open. The entire room had been turned upside down, and the bedding slashed to ribbons. His clothes were strewn about, with some of them shredded. The beautiful furniture had been tossed about and broken as if a tornado had entered the room.

As he looked about in dismay, he saw that a note had been left on the bed. It had been written on a sheet of Rachel Humphries' stationary, with bold lettering that had been angrily scrawled across it.

> I have waited for you long enough priest. Either you come to me tomorrow, or I will start playing with the people in the hotel. The choice is yours.

Getting out of the clothes he had spent the night in, Randy changed into the few items of fresh clothing that he could still find. Carefully, he put his crucifix around his neck. As always, he wore the St. Michael medallion under his clothing.

Before continuing, he knelt down in prayer:

> "Dear God, help me to find the strength and courage to face Gorshault. Give me the wisdom and understanding I will need to resolve this crisis. Whatever the outcome may be, however, let it be done according to your will. Amen."

He continued to kneel in silence for a while. He felt that all too often, people were so busy talking to God, that they never gave Him an opportunity to reply. Accordingly, he always followed each prayer with a period of silence wherein he tried to clear his mind of all thoughts.

Putting fresh batteries in his lamp, he entered the passageways and resolutely made his way towards Gorshault. The heavy wooden door that had stood ajar at the exit of the underground library had been thrown aside with such force that it had shattered against the stone wall.

Randy entered the underground passageways. He soon found himself at the entrance to Gorshault's palace. From this point on, he had no idea of what to expect. He stepped into the entry hall and looked around. The various sculptures along the walls sent shivers down his spine. Their facial expressions glittered with a sense of malice that almost felt tangible. The realism with which they portrayed the various scenes of carnage that circled the room, was enough to make Randy feel nauseous. The walls glowed red, casting an eerie hue across his hands and face. Randy had expected to find Gorshault waiting for him, and was surprised not to find him. He was startled when a deep voice seemed to boom from the walls themselves.

"Take the straight path, and you will find me."

There was a large, arched doorway directly ahead of him. He stepped around the central pillar and walked through the arches. A large expansive hallway lay before him. After seeing the entry hall, he had thought that perhaps Gorshault's palace might be impressive, but this was overwhelming. A large broad flight of stairs led down into the hallway, which was roughly the size of a football field. Two columns of pillars went down either side, and supported the arched roof, which was at least thirty feet high. It was like stepping into the palace of some ancient king, or emperor. Again, everything was made out of the same dark red rock that made up the entryway. The deep gloss of the stone scattered the light from Randy's lamp throughout the hall. The sinister feeling of the place grew rather than diminished. Randy could not shake the feeling that the stones themselves were watching him, scrutinizing his every move.

He strode down the stairs into the hall. In contrast to the ornate entry hall, this hall was devoid of any carvings. Indeed, it needed none. The sheer vastness of the hall was more than enough to create a feeling of awe. Gorshault certainly had an eye for architecture.

The glowing of the rock had become bright enough that Randy turned off his lamp. The glow was not only strong enough to see by, but it seemed to permeate everything. Even though Randy had worn his priestly collar, along with the appropriate black clothing, when he looked down at himself, everything looked blood red.

Randy began to shiver as the air continued to turn colder with each step. His footsteps echoed throughout the hallway, taking several seconds to die away. He began to feel as a beggar would that had crept into the palace of a high and mighty lord.

As he walked down the hallway, he saw several arched doorways on the sides, all illuminated with the same eerie red glow. Some opened into passageways that continued on into the distance, whereas others opened onto broad stairways that led further down into the bowels of the mountain.

He continued on to the end of the hall where large double doors stood closed in front of him. Each door appeared several feet across, and at least a dozen feet high. They were made of gold, and were exquisitely formed. Each one had the shapes of dolphins embossed on them that appeared so life-like, that they seemed to swim in the gold of the doors. Even though they were magnificent, Randy couldn't help but notice that they seemed very much out of place with the sinister feel of the palace. They looked to have been molded by an artist who had had veneration for life, and was in possession of the skill to infuse his work with that love. They were certainly not the work of a demon who delighted in fear and death.

Randy was trying to figure out how to open the doors, when they began to silently open inwards on their own. As they opened, Randy saw they were almost a foot thick. He waited patiently for them to open all the way before he continued. As the doors parted, Randy could feel the frigid air that flowed from between them. A smell of rotting flesh filled his nostrils and he had to swallow hard to keep his stomach from rising. He had no doubt that Gorshault was just ahead of him.

As he stepped through the open doors, Randy found himself in a large throne room. It was circular with a large domed roof. It was completely empty, except for a large dais surrounded by a half dozen steps. On the top was a large throne made of the now familiar red rock. Seated on the throne was Gorshault. Slowly, Randy walked the twenty paces it took to get to the bottom step of the dais. He looked up and gazed upon the demon.

It was difficult to make out what Gorshault looked like. He wrapped himself in a shadow that permitted no light to enter, not even the reddish glow of the rock. The only thing Randy could make out were two red eyes that seemed to regard him from within the shadow.

"Greetings, Priest. I am delighted that you decided to accept my invitation."

Gorshault spoke in a deep, but quiet voice. A voice that didn't need to be raised in order to demand attention. Every word conveyed a sense of authority that not only filled the air, but also appeared in the listener's mind.

"You didn't leave me much choice," answered Randy.

"Even so, a lesser man would have fled, putting as much distance between me and himself as possible. At least you have the courage to come and face me. Even though I have been cheated out of the sport of the chase, I suppose your actions are to be expected from someone who is supposed to destroy me."

"How do you know I'm supposed to destroy you?" Randy tried in vain to see through the darkness that surrounded Gorshault.

"Mortals are trapped within the linear progression of time. Immortal beings such as myself exist outside of time, and are able to view glimpses of both the past and future. Granted, the future is not absolute. It can vary in its details according to the actions of the individuals involved. Your being here, however, was an event that I foresaw with unusual clarity. How you could possibly aspire to destroy me, however, is somewhat of a mystery. I suspect now that my concerns have been groundless. It is strange, however, that you do not shake in terror as other mortals do when I confront them."

"My faith gives me strength."

"Your faith." Gorshault laughed, then snorted in disgust. "Your faith will not help you here. This is my domain, and by entering it, you have placed yourself completely in *my* power. *I* reign supreme here." The demon shifted on his throne, and Randy watched as shades of black tumbled over each other, reforming the hazy image. The eyes remained vigilant.

"Only God reigns supreme, demon. If he wished, he could destroy this entire palace with you in it."

Gorshault laughed heartily. "Indeed he could, if he wished to. But he won't. God decreed that mortals should have the freedom of choice. For him to come down here and destroy me would violate his own decree. He would be removing from the world a possible temptation for mortals, thereby limiting their choices."

"For an evil spirit, you seem to have a great deal of knowledge about God."

Gorshault laughed again. "Is that all you think of me? That I was once a mere mortal whose spirit now haunts the earth? Randy, you disappoint me. *I* am an ***angel***."

Slowly, Gorshault rose from his throne. The shadows began to swirl and melt away. Randy stood transfixed as he beheld a towering figure, at least ten feet tall, standing on the dais. Hardened muscles, like cords of steel, wrapped around the arms and legs. Instead of the misshapen, beast-like creature that Randy expected to see, he looked at a physique that would have been the envy of a Greek god. A thick powerful neck supported a head that was equally magnificent with sharply chiseled features exhibiting perfect symmetry. Except for long golden-colored hair that flowed to his shoulders, the blood red flesh was devoid of any body hair and glistened in the soft light that emanated from the walls. Indeed, Randy could well believe that he was looking upon an angel were it not for the eyes. The deep-set red eyes glowed like hot coals, smoldering in their sockets. They continued to transfix Randy with evil and malice. He cowered at the bottom of the dais.

"This is how you may worship me," exulted Gorshault as he raised his arms.

Randy shook internally, but remained resolute. "I worship only God."

Gorshault let out a roar of rage that thundered throughout his palace. The stones trembled and shook with his anger. Randy covered his ears to protect them from the painful blast. "Then this is how you will fear me!"

Gorshault's arms lengthened until they reached down to the floor. The muscles grew ever larger and harder until they seemed to be chiseled out of the very rock upon which Gorshault stood. Sharp red claws scraped the rock upon which they rested. The legs bowed outward from the tension of oversized muscles that knotted around them. Thick red fur grew out from his back and arms. A bestial snout covered his face with fangs that sprouted ever longer until they hung below his chin. Drops of venomous saliva shimmered in the light as they dripped to the floor and lay steaming on the rock. Puffs of nauseous steam spouted through small slits in the center of his face. Thick ridges of flesh surround his eyes and covered his forehead.

Randy did indeed fear the horror that stood over him, able to swat him out of existence with but a flick of one of its monstrous arms. He turned inward, and drawing courage from the faith inside of him, continued to question Gorshault. "How is it that an angel is to be found here, deep underground?"

"I joined Lucifer in his rebellion against God. Alas, Lucifer miscalculated. He was not yet ready to challenge God's power."

Randy had indeed misjudged Gorshault, and thought him to be an evil spirit, albeit a very powerful one. As a priest, he felt confident about his ability to cast out evil spirits. But a fallen angel? How could he possibly stand against such a being?

"How could Lucifer have thought himself to be more than his creator," asked Randy.

"That is not so unlikely." Gorshault settled his beast-like form back on the throne after calming down. "The creation can sometimes become more powerful than the creator. Take a look at your own world. A computer is far more capable than the minds that conceived it. With the advances being made in artificial intelligence, is it so inconceivable that computers may some day control humanity? And, for that matter, who's to say that Lucifer hasn't proven himself more powerful?"

"Surely you joke!" Randy shivered in the cold.

"Not at all. Look at your world's history. Look at how the forces of evil have, time and time again, influenced the direction of events. Beginning with the temptation of Eve, and continuing onward with the corruption of Sodom and Gomorrah, the brutality of Ghengis Khan, the betrayal of Christ by Judas, the depravity of the Roman Empire, the establishment of communist totalitarian empires, the genocide of the Jews by Hitler. I could go on and on."

"I agree that evil has had its brief moments of victory. But each time, the evil was eventually rooted out."

"Lucifer and his forces have suffered setbacks," conceded Gorshault. "But they have never been rooted out."

"I can't help but notice that when you refer to 'Lucifer and his forces,' you do so in such a fashion, that one would think you don't consider yourself a part of them.".

"You are perceptive. Indeed, I chose not to take up with Lucifer. The fool had already miscalculated once by beginning his rebellion against God, and I had no desire to be involved in any of his further machinations. While violence may on occasion be useful, I no longer take the delight in it that Satan does. Centuries ago, I too meddled in mankind's history. I was the advisor to the King of Atlantis, and helped fuel their desire for power into an obsession that eventually destroyed them. The golden doors you were admiring once served as the entryway into the King's palace. Once the kingdom had sunk to the ocean floor, they no longer had need of them, and I appropriated them for my own abode. Since then, I have tried to enjoy a quiet existence, and have only occasionally been bothered by mortals. Indeed, you are the first mortal to enter my halls. No one else has dared."

"Why did you build this magnificent palace?"

"When I found that I did not derive the intense pleasure from the destruction of Atlantis as I had been led to believe by Lucifer, I decided I would prefer not to be bothered by the petty squabbles of mortals. Expending a great deal of power, I constructed this palace out of a material that I helped the Atlanteans to develop. Not only is it virtually impervious to any power you mortals have discovered, it is also a barricade to any supernatural force that might be directed against me. A perfect way for me to insure that our confrontation will not be interfered with."

"It's also a perfect prison," observed Randy. "I'm surprised you made no effort to keep me from once again trapping you, as you were trapped centuries ago by the Spanish missionary priest."

"Trust me, once I found myself freed, I made the effort to construct a second exit, a feat that requires work on both the inside and outside of these walls. Something I could not do while trapped on the inside."

"You certainly are a wealth of information. Why?"

"For the same reason you have not made any hostile moves towards me. It is always wise to study one's adversary first, determine strengths and weaknesses. And who knows, I might even turn you into an ally, and you will worship me instead."

"I remember your recent actions far too well, Gorshault. I have no wish to end up as Rachel did. I doubt if anything you say can change my opinion."

"What makes you think I care what your opinion is?" growled Gorshault angrily. "After all, what are you but a worthless mortal?"

"I am one of God's creations, just as you are," replied Randy softly.

Gorshault fell silent at that, as if lost in thought. His head momentarily bowed as he crossed his fingers in his lap. It was several seconds before he spoke again.

"Rachel was a mistake. I was anxious to be released, and in my desperation, I turned her into a creature that benefited neither one of us. She was a very intelligent and beautiful woman. I never could convince her that I cared for her."

Once again Gorshault became silent for some time before continuing. Randy noticed that the eyes had lost some of their fire. "I digress, Priest. You state that nothing I say will make you change your mind. What if I showed you how vain your struggle against the forces of evil are? Instead of listening to me, you could see with your own eyes, and make your own judgment. Will you trust me enough to take a little trip with me? I give you my word that I will not harm you."

"What do you propose?" asked Randy cautiously.

"With my assistance, we will leave these cumbersome bodies behind, and look at your world as it now is."

It was Randy's turn to pause in thought. To say that Randy was flabbergasted at the suggestion would be an understatement of gigantic proportions. He did not particularly enjoy the idea of putting himself in Gorshault's power. The opportunity might, however, present him with more insight into the workings of Gorshault's mind. Besides, Randy did not delude himself. He realized that Gorshault could crush him like an ant anytime he wished. Not that Randy was particularly concerned with his safety. He had absolute faith that Gorshault could do nothing to harm him. Certainly, Gorshault could destroy Randy's body, but as long as Randy did not willingly give in to Gorshault, Randy's soul would always remain outside of Gorshault's reach. After careful consideration, he felt that the possible benefits far outweighed the risks. He breathed a silent prayer to Saint Michael, then raised his head to look up at Gorshault.

"What would you have me do?"

"You are a brave one. I have to admit, I find you very intriguing, for a mortal. Sit at the bottom of the steps, and recline back so that your body will not be harmed once you have left it. Then relax, and try to empty your mind of all thoughts.

Now, without moving your body physically, imagine holding out your hand for me to grasp."

Randy did as instructed, trying to banish all apprehension from his mind. He imagined raising up his arm and holding out his hand. He felt a firm and powerful grip take that hand, and with a tug, Randy suddenly found himself looking down at his own body. How frail and insignificant he looked, lying like a rag doll that had been carelessly left on the floor. He looked around for Gorshault, but saw only a shadowy form on the throne that was hunched over. He could hear Gorshault's voice enter his thoughts.

"You can no longer physically see or hear me," Gorshault explained. "If you wish to communicate with me, you must direct your thoughts towards me. I will remain at your side. Now imagine that I am once again taking your hand."

Randy did so, and could again feel the same powerful grip take hold. He marveled as he whisked through Gorshault's palace, out through the mountainside, and into the world.

Chapter Eight - Conversion

Randy exulted in the freedom of being released from the constraints of his physical body. He could go anywhere he wished in the instant that it took to formulate the thought. The whole world lay beneath him, but not in a physical, three-dimensional sense. Rather, it was revealed in his consciousness. He could either look at it in its entirety, or if he desired, he could focus in on a specific event and scrutinize it. He experienced not only the limitless mobility of being freed from his body, but also a heightened sense of awareness. He was able to take in multitudes of events at the same time. He couldn't understand how anyone could experience this and not be overwhelmed by the beauty of the spirit. He directed his thoughts towards Gorshault to convey his reactions.

Beautiful you think, came the reply. *Let me show you another side.*

They whisked down into the treatment room of a clinic. On the stainless-steel table, lay a woman in her mid- twenties, resting. The nurses were cleaning up, as though a procedure had just taken place.

Look in the pan over there, came Gorshault's thoughts.

Randy looked where he was directed. Amidst the blood, there was a small human fetus only a couple of inches in length. It was already well formed, complete with tiny fingers and toes. He could sense that the heart had just stopped beating.

This woman felt that she did not have the time to deal with a child, explained Gorshault. *It would have been too disruptive to her career and her free-spirited single lifestyle. So in the name of "freedom of choice," she opted to have the life within her killed, and have the body of her child removed from her womb so she wouldn't be inconvenienced. It is this same rationalization that is now being used to argue for assisted suicide and euthanasia. It won't be long before this cheapening of human life is used to justify who will be allowed to live and who must die. The eventual outcome will be a society where an elitist group of individuals makes life and death decisions based on their own sets of values. And I can assure you that it won't be the forces of good making those decisions.*

They left the clinic behind, and Randy found himself in a high school classroom where students were learning computer skills.

Notice the two students in the back, suggested Gorshault.

Randy did so, and saw that they were on the Internet. The material on the screen, however, was not what he would have expected to see in an academic setting. Both students were staring at pornographic material. One of them was sending an electronic message to the purveyor, answering the advertisement for models and expressing her desire to become involved. The teacher, at her desk at the front of the classroom, was totally oblivious to what was happening.

We can now reach young people in school, explained Gorshault, *cultivating their baser desires. The Internet has given us access to people who would never have had any exposure to this type of material. The use of the Internet is also allowing more people to have home offices, take classes from their computers, and so on.*

What's wrong with more people staying in their homes? asked Randy.

From my point of view, nothing. The home computer does not lend itself to family activities. It is strictly an individual past time. Not only does it lessen the interaction family members have with each other, helping to further disintegrate the family unit, it also helps to isolate individuals from the rest of society. Envision a future where most people work, go to school, and indulge in recreation, all in front of their computer screen. These people will develop no social skills, and have absolutely no contact with the world outside them, except for what is fed to them through their computers. Again, what a perfect opportunity for an elitist group of individuals to completely control society.

They left the classroom, and Randy was surrounded by a rain forest. Lush trees and undergrowth dripped with moisture that steamed in the afternoon sun. Amidst the vegetation, there were remnants of old shacks and dilapidated buildings. The various forest denizens scurried about the relics as the jungle slowly took back its own.

We are in South America, at the site of a mass suicide that took place years ago, came Gorshault's thoughts. *Hundreds of men, women, and children drank a cyanide-laced mixture that killed them. Those who did not wish to participate, were forced by the others. They had all come here as followers of a "so called disciple" that eventually preached* to them the necessity of suicide to reach heaven. *In recent decades, these false prophets have been able to lure more and more willing followers to their deaths, all in the name of religion.*

Again they sped away, this time to a run down abandoned building that was being used by a gang. All of the members were children, ranging in ages from twelve, to the upper teens. Many were using drugs, and there was a proliferation of knives and firearms in possession of the youths. Rats milled about at the edge of the gathering, seeing if they could scavenge anything from the piles of refuse that were scattered about the floor. The air stank from the filth and human waste that had accumulated in the building. One small boy held a syringe while another tied a giant rubber band around his arm.

Many of these children have no other place to go, thought Gorshault to Randy. *Your society is now structured in such a way that both parents have to work, either to meet their financial obligations, or maintain an affluent lifestyle at the expense of their family. There are also many single-parent households that are a result of the violent death of one of the parents, the desertion of one of the parents, or caused by the growing divorce rate. This is further compounded by a trend in the workplace by many major companies that demand extra hours of their employees, often without extra pay so that these employees can demonstrate their loyalty to the company above all else; loyalty that they are told is crucial to advancement, or even being able to keep their jobs. These children no longer have a family that they can go home to. Corporate greed has decreed that the welfare of the employees be last on their list of priorities. Companies no longer care about what they are doing to their employees, or to society. In desperation, these children join gangs in order to fill the void in their lives caused by the lack of parental involvement. These gangs, in turn, expose them to a life of crime, murder, and decadence.*

Off they went again, to a laboratory filled with research animals. Researchers were busy studying data they were obtaining from the dissection of a monkey that still lay on the table.

Science is always a wonderful tool that can be used to tempt mankind into areas of research that can be potentially self-destructive, explained Gorshault. *Here, they are studying the possibilities of cloning, having performed several experiments with the animals you see here. It is a foregone conclusion that the experiments will eventually take place with human beings. In the name of "science," natural human evolution will be altered. How long before humans will be manufactured "to order," to fill certain duties and "needs" within society? The ultimate way to control mankind.*

I have shown you just a small sampling of the fruits of evil resulting from your own society. I could take you to other areas of the world where dictators are responsible for a multitude of atrocities. The forces of Lucifer have indeed gained footholds within your society, many of which will result in his total control of the world. Your time is past, priest.

No, thought Randy to Gorshault, *you are wrong. Yes, there are problems in society, but there is also great good. Now it's my turn. Let me be the guide.*

As you wish, priest. Just focus your thoughts on where you would go.

Randy did so, and they left the laboratory behind. They came to an amusement park on an island, in the middle of a large lake. A roller coaster twisted and corkscrewed along the shore. The park was filled with rides of all descriptions that spun, flew, sped, scared, and allowed their riders to enjoy experiences not available anywhere else. On one of the water rides, a somewhat shaky looking twelve-year-old girl was buckling in. Her clothes were too loose on her, and she wore a woolen hat despite the heat. Not a strand of hair could be seen sticking out from underneath the hat. Her brown eyes stared out from hollow looking sockets, but her smile radiated to those around her.

This little girl is dying of cancer, explained Randy to Gorshault. *Several major companies and individuals all donated money, so she could fulfill her wish and come here to Wonder Island. None of the people who donated know her personally. It was out of compassion for her plight, and others like her, that they wished to help. Projects such as these have gained national media attention, and more people are beginning to understand the joy they can provide someone who is facing a hopeless situation.*

Randy continued the journey to the nursery of a private home, where a father was busy comforting a crying baby. The love in the father's eyes as he looked at the child, helped to calm the infant, eventually causing the baby to giggle cheerfully as the father made funny faces.

This man is a parishioner in my own congregation, thought Randy to Gorshault. *He and his wife were unable to conceive a child of their own. They possessed such a love of children, that they adopted this baby from a country that is less fortunate than ours. You only have to look at the man's face to realize the love he has for this baby. Adoption is becoming a more popular choice with many couples, allowing children to grow up in homes filled with love rather than being isolated in orphanages.*

They left the nursery, and Randy took Gorshault to an operating room in a hospital. The room shone with antiseptic cleanliness. A woman lay on the operating table, her eyes wide with concern, as the nurses finalized their preparations. *This woman heard of a small child that will die unless the child receives a bone marrow transplant. Moved by her compassion, she had herself tested, and found out that her bone marrow was a good match for the child. As a result, this woman is facing surgery, so the child will have a chance to live. A child she had never met until just recently. More and more people are stepping forward to become organ donors, so that others can find renewed hope of life.*

They went to an older neighborhood in a large city. Small frame houses lined the street, with graffiti generously applied to walls and fences. In sharp contrast, the lawns were mostly well tended, and the homes looked clean, despite the flakes of paint that were working loose on the majority of them. There was a small restaurant on the corner that enjoyed a brisk business despite the locale.

This is the scene, where every Thanksgiving, the restaurant owner sets up buffet lines and feeds the less fortunate, explained Randy. *He donates all the food himself, and many families volunteer their time to help feed the poor. There are literally hundreds of private institutions and individuals that provide food for the poor, or operate shelters where the poor and homeless can come to receive assistance on a daily basis. These volunteers are not motivated by profit, but by their love and compassion for others.*

I agree that the world has many problems, continued Randy, *but there are countless examples of people making selfless sacrifices on behalf of others. These sacrifices are not sensational enough to merit the media attention that human tragedies receive, but their contribution to society is immeasurable. Love and compassion not only continue to exist in the modern world, they have flourished to the point of bringing down totalitarian empires.*

Tell me, Gorshault, is it possible to travel to a past occurrence? asked Randy

Yes, but you must have a specific occurrence in mind, preferably one that you are personally familiar with, answered Gorshault. *While in the present, one has an overview of all events, making it relatively simple to find what one is looking for: much as we have done. When you look to the past, however, events become vague and are more difficult to isolate.*

Randy concentrated, and they both found themselves back at Shady Valley, eighteen years ago when Thunder was being laid to rest. As Randy saw himself crying by the grave while helping to lower Thunder's body into it, the full memory of the event flooded into him, opening a heart-ache that had never healed. He saw the rope burns forming in his hands as he struggled to keep the heavy body from falling into the grave, sweat making the ropes slippery to hold onto. Father Brian was standing at the head of the grave, waiting until the body had been settled in place so he could say some appropriate words. Ellen stood off to the side, quiet, with a glazed look in her eyes as she stared at the scene before her.

Gorshault, you have hurt a great many people throughout your existence, but have you ever given thought to the pain that your actions have inflicted on others?

What would I care about the feelings of mortals, answered Gorshault indignantly.

You might find it educational, responded Randy. *Or are you afraid?*

Afraid? Gorshault does not fear the feelings of mortals. What do you propose?

Down there, the burial of my dog Thunder is taking place. Out of love, he risked his life to save mine from Rachel. Afterwards, he grew sick and died. Link your mind to mine, and experience with me the emotions of the loss.

You realize the risk you are taking, warned Gorshault. *By opening your mind to me, you will give me complete control. With but a mere thought, I could end your existence.*

I am not afraid. You won't hurt me.

Randy was more than willing to take the risk. In the exchange of thoughts they already experienced, Randy had caught glimpses of Gorshault's mind, and was convinced that evil did not completely dominate him. Gorshault had doubts about his course of action, but felt he no longer had any alternatives.

Randy opened his mind, and felt Gorshault's conscienceness flood into his own. As Randy had expected, it was a two-way exchange, and he found he was able to search Gorshault's memories as well. Randy marveled at the beauty of Gorshault's existence prior to Lucifer's corruption. Randy had experienced closeness with God as a priest, but compared to the personal relationship Gorshault had shared, Randy's was like a barren wasteland. When Lucifer started his whisperings, Gorshault listened out of curiosity. Lucifer's reasoning had a logic to it that appealed to Gorshault's desire for structure and order in the world. When the rebellion came, Gorshault found himself being numbered among the rebels. The power that Michael had wielded on behalf of God was astounding, and left Gorshault dazed with the situation he found himself in.

Realizing how wrong Lucifer had been, he struck out on his own. Too proud to admit his part in the rebellion had been a mistake, he meddled in human affairs somewhat, but as with the rebellion, he found Lucifer's ideas and tactics to be less than satisfying.

He eventually built his underground dwelling in the hopes of being able to exist in isolation, and not be bothered by anyone or anything. Yes, he had killed, and done so quite gruesomely. There again, it was out of what he felt was necessity in order to protect his privacy.

He had been so informative and cooperative to Randy, because he almost wished he would be destroyed. His existence ceased to fulfill any purpose, and over the centuries, his freedom became more and more restricted. He created a hideous body to better instill fear in humans. Over the centuries, the body appeared more and more repulsive, and Gorshault soon found himself trapped in it. He could change it or leave it for short periods of time, but had lost the ability to once again be a free spirit. Indeed, Randy could sense that Gorshault was starting to weaken, and would need to return to his body soon. Randy found himself pitying Gorshault. Over the years, Randy nursed a hatred for him, considering him to be the cause of a great deal of pain in Randy's life. Randy was now able to let go of that hatred, and felt as if a great burden had been lifted from him.

Gorshault also found the sharing of memories to be more than he expected. Pride caused him to look upon humans with disdain, and prevented him from considering them as much more than mere animals. By going through Randy's thoughts and memories, he realized that the only thing that once set him apart from humanity, was his closeness to God. Once that was lost, he ceased to be different.

The loss of Thunder that he shared with Randy was far more intense than he had expected. He would never have expected the depth of human emotion that he experienced, especially for the loss of what he considered to be nothing more than a mere pet. Indeed, he thought to himself, God *had* created humans in his own image. For the first time, Gorshault realized the pain he had caused countless individuals throughout the centuries. The realization was overwhelming as once again Gorshault experienced compassion, something he had not allowed himself to feel since before Lucifer's rebellion.

He felt himself growing weak from the extended absence from his body. He was tempted not to return, to see if perhaps his existence would come to an end. He realized, however, that that would also spell Randy's doom, and he could no longer permit that. He owed Randy a great debt, and could not let any harm come to him. Taking a firm hold on Randy's spirit, he sped across the short distance of time and space, back to his throne room.

Chapter Nine - Repentance

As Randy's spirit settled back into his body, he opened his eyes and stood up. He turned to face Gorshault, and looked at him in a new light. The loathing he once felt was replaced with pity for a misguided creature, who had once been near the pinnacle of existence, then tumbled down to the depths of despair.

"I would wish that you did indeed possess the power to destroy me." Gorshault spoke softly, his giant form hunched over. "But I now know that you do not. I did, however, foresee correctly that my existence as I knew it would come to an end. I regret the pain that I have caused you. Please leave me. I assure you, I will never trouble humanity again."

"No." Randy held out his hand. "Come with me and let us leave this evil place together. Take my hand and walk with me to the outside. There, we can kneel side by side and pray to God for forgiveness. If someone as insignificant as myself can forgive you, I know that God in his greatness surely will."

"You are not insignificant, Randy. Do not underestimate yourself. I will do as you ask. I no longer have anything to loose. If in his wrath, God smites me down, the burden of my existence will at least be over."

The shadow that was Gorshault rose, and came down the steps to Randy. Randy continued to hold out his hand, and a beast-like clawed paw was laid in it. Grasping Gorshault firmly, Randy led him out of the throne room, and into the great hall. Slowly, Gorshault's great frame bent over, they made their way out. The once proud shoulders sagged as he painfully shuffled, step by step. The bright fire that had raged in his eyes was now diminished, and tears flowed down his face. Only a faint flicker remained. When they reached the chamber just outside the entry hall, Gorshault faltered. "I am strangely weakened, I don't know why. I can not make it any further."

"Then let us kneel here, and pray together."

Shakily, they both fell to their knees.

"Dear God, I bring to you Gorshault, who was once your servant. His sins are many. Nevertheless, I pray to you on his behalf, and beg of you to forgive him. Please take him back to be one of your children once again. Have mercy on him. Amen."

Randy had no idea of what to expect, but had simply followed his urge to pray. He waited on his knees with Gorshault for what seemed an interminable time, and was about to get up, when he saw a bright light start to fill up the chamber. It grew in brilliance until the chamber was unbearably bright. Gorshault's shadow slowly dissipated, revealing his features. Much to Randy's amazement, Gorshault's beast-like features gradually transformed into those of a man. As the transformation progressed, Gorshault became translucent, and Randy could no longer feel the hand that lay in his.

Two shapes began to materialize before him. Their beauty was beyond words, and Randy found himself speechless with wonder, as he realized they were both angels. Even though they had human forms, they appeared to consist of radiant light, whiter than the stars. Their smiles gave him a comfort he had not experienced since he was a child, being held in his father's arms. The closest one to him spoke.

"I am Michael, the archangel. Gorshault, do we understand that it is your intent to repent, and to return to us? I warn you that your penance will be arduous, and the road back, very difficult."

"It is my intention," answered Gorshault firmly.

"Gabriel, take Gorshault back with you."

The angel to the rear came forward, and took Gorshault's hand from Randy. They began to fade, when Gorshault shouted, "Wait."

Gorshault turned to Randy. "Thank you for helping me find myself again. If I am able, rest assured I will always look out for you." Gorshault turned back to Gabriel, and together they faded from sight.

Michael remained in the chamber with Randy. The angel was an embodiment of radiance that made him difficult to see. His form conveyed a sense of eternal youth and vigor.

"The rejoicing in heaven will be as never before. Thank you for bringing our brother back to us. You do indeed possess a special power, but not the type that Gorshault expected. You are a priest. Accordingly, you have the ability to empathize with others, and help them achieve a conversion of heart. Use your power well."

Michael began to fade, but his voice continued.

"You have a birthday next week. As a token of our appreciation, we will have a special gift for you. Farewell."

Overcome with the intensity of his emotions, Randy remained in the chamber on his knees, whispering prayers of thanksgiving.

A week later, Randy was home with his parents for a birthday party. Fred and Janet had also come over, and brought the twins with them. For the first time in eighteen years, they were all able to celebrate with true joy. The evil that had haunted them for years was gone.

After his confrontation with Gorshault, Randy had gone back to his hotel room to find his parents waiting for him. They heard of Randy's accidents from Father Joe, and realized where Randy had probably gone. Randy briefly related to them what had happened, feeling uncomfortable about sharing the details. Hoping to prevent anyone else from stumbling upon Gorshault's palace, he took his father with him into the passageways, to figure out how to block up the entrance permanently. They found, however, that they couldn't get any further than the passageway that connected the two houses. The passageway was intact, but where the natural cave had veered off to the chamber and Gorshault's palace, solid rock blocked their progress. It was almost as if the cave had never existed.

Randy had just blown out the candles on his cake when the doorbell rang. Jake went to answer it, and came back with a large basket and a puzzled look on his face. "No one was at the door, but I found this on our door step, with a note that reads 'For Randy.'"

Curious, Randy stepped over to take a look. There was a blanket covering the basket. Pulling it aside, he found a small St. Bernard puppy that looked happily up at him.

Even after so many years, Randy recognized the look in the puppy's eyes. Gratefully, he picked the puppy up and hugged him. Tears of happiness flowed down his cheeks as the puppy licked his face. Thunder had been returned to him.